Praise for *Nightingale*

'A glorious, glass-sharp novel, raw and   and beautiful. Every sentence Elvery writ   ...ent. *Nightingale* reminded me what great fiction can reveal to us.' **Robbie Arnott**

'As one would expect in a novel featuring Florence Nightingale, this is a book about war and sacrifice and gendered expectations, but it's also about ambition, desire, time, the drive to be useful and the endlessness of grief. Elvery's characters feel conjured, rather than written: mystical and physically, achingly human at the same time. *Nightingale* is a remarkable work of invention, scalpel sharp and heroically tender.' **Emily Maguire**

'Original, brilliant and wise. *Nightingale* shows the precarious humanity behind any historical myth, and honours in tender, vivid prose the physical and metaphysical dimensions of past lives. A beautiful achievement.' **Gail Jones**

'Elvery rips the heart out of historical events and leaves it beating on the page. The writing is incandescent. A generous and compassionate account of a history reclaimed. I will be forever haunted by this book.' **Kris Kneen**

Praise for *Ordinary Matter*

'*Ordinary Matter* is, in the best sense, a surprising collection: intellectually ambitious; offering unexpected digressions and deliberately odd conjunctions ... This engaging and unusual collection will consolidate Elvery's reputation as a writer of fine short stories.' ***Australian Book Review***

'*Ordinary Matter* is not what it says on the tin, it's better. Fully charged and slightly unstable; an element with surplus electrons, ready to jump.' ***The Age***

'In their sheer variousness and imaginative verve, [these stories] kick science out of the laboratory and into a broader, messier human milieu.' ***The Saturday Paper***

'What is clear from reading *Ordinary Matter* is that Laura Elvery is a writer whose talents are anything but ordinary.' ***The AU Review***

'Luminescent, sensitive ... [and] skilful.' ***Books+Publishing***

'Elegant, wise and humming with insight – this sublime collection proves that Elvery is in a class of her own.' **Toni Jordan**

'These stories gently and beautifully track the outward ripples of these women's scientific achievements, through the years and across decades. An experimental and literary triumph.' **Ceridwen Dovey**

'A beautifully crafted and moving collection of stories about women who change history while struggling against its constraints.' **Abigail Ulman**

Praise for *Trick of the Light*

'Delightful ... A complex emotional intimacy is present in all of Elvery's stories, but it's her inventive characters meeting original circumstances that makes *Trick of the Light* that rare thing: a page-turning short fiction collection.' ***The Saturday Paper***

'Elvery's debut reads like a triumph of excavation – a collection in which dark matter is exposed and subsequently transformed ... An intriguing and powerful new writer.' ***Overland***

'Elvery has a good eye for detail and her observation of human nature is astute.' ***ArtsHub***

'An assured collection, insightful and moving.' ***Brisbane News***

'Radiant, accomplished and exquisitely written, this is an outstanding collection.' **Ryan O'Neill**

'*Trick of the Light* is at times haunting and poetic, other times bright and sharp, and always memorable and hopeful ... This thoroughly profound, bold and playful debut pulled me along and pulled me apart.' **Brooke Davis**

Laura Elvery is the author of *Trick of the Light* and *Ordinary Matter*, which won the 2021 USQ Steele Rudd Award for a Short Story Collection, and was shortlisted for the Queensland Premier's Award for a Work of State Significance and the 2022 Barbara Jefferis Award. Laura has won the Josephine Ulrick Prize for Literature, the Margaret River Short Story Competition, the Neilma Sidney Short Story Prize and the Fair Australia Prize for Fiction. *Nightingale* is her first novel.

NIGHTINGALE

LAURA ELVERY

UQP

First published 2025 by University of Queensland Press
PO Box 6042, St Lucia, Queensland 4067 Australia

The University of Queensland Press (UQP) acknowledges the Traditional Owners and their custodianship of the lands on which UQP operates. We pay our respects to their Ancestors and their descendants, who continue cultural and spiritual connections to Country. We recognise their valuable contributions to Australian and global society.

uqp.com.au
reception@uqp.com.au

Copyright © Laura Elvery 2025
The moral rights of the author have been asserted.

This book is copyright. Except for private study, research, criticism or reviews, as permitted under the Copyright Act, no part of this book may be reproduced, stored in a retrieval system, or transmitted in any form or by any means without prior written permission. Enquiries should be made to the publisher.

Cover design by Josh Durham, Design by Committee
Cover illustration by Josh Durham and Alamy Stock Photo
Author photograph by Trenton Porter
Typeset in 12.5/18.5 pt Adobe Caslon Pro by Post Pre-press Group, Brisbane
Printed in Australia by McPherson's Printing Group

The epigraph by TS Eliot on p. xi is taken from 'Little Gidding', in his *Collected Poems 1909–1962*, published by Faber & Faber Ltd. Reproduced with permission of Faber & Faber Ltd.

University of Queensland Press is assisted by the Australian Government through Creative Australia, its principal arts investment and advisory body.

University of Queensland Press is assisted by the Queensland Government through Arts Queensland.

A catalogue record for this book is available from the National Library of Australia.

ISBN 978 0 7022 6587 7 (pbk)
ISBN 978 0 7022 6745 1 (epdf)
ISBN 978 0 7022 6746 8 (epub)

University of Queensland Press uses papers that are natural, renewable and recyclable products made from wood grown in well-managed forests and other controlled sources. The logging and manufacturing processes conform to the environmental regulations of the country of origin.

For Theo

*We shall not cease from exploration
And the end of all our exploring
Will be to arrive where we started
And know the place for the first time.*
– TS Eliot

Struggle must make a noise.
– Florence Nightingale

Prologue

The Acropolis of Athens
June 1850

One boy had no boots on at all, just a strip of dirt around his ankle that reminded Florence of a scummy line around the edge of a white bath. For some time she'd been studying him and his friends playing near the Parthenon. She counted five boys and was drawn to the one with a scrap of red cloth tied around his wrist. At first, she thought they were playing a complicated game, one that was alien to her and special to them. And so she had stopped strolling along the stones, where their voices were calling to one another, and she came to rest against a tree. She stood very still. Getting the details and intricacies of the game correct would mean she could write another holiday letter to Aunt Mai and describe them. The way they were throwing their bodies around, jeering and laughing, rushing at something in the centre of their circle. A white ball, which was not odd at all. She would tell Aunt Mai what she and the Bracebridges had eaten for lunch (fava, horiatiki salata, psarakia, lamb), tell her about the smell of bread baking, the mucky dampness of the wet stone all around, the puddles from an overnight shower that lay near her feet. Above her, the sky was a joyful, unbroken blue.

Then from the middle of the boys' circle the white ball began to rise, and her mind narrowed as she tried to keep up with what she was seeing. The ball was rising too slowly to be something that had been kicked up from the earth. And the word that came to her began with the shape of her mouth, which was making an *O*.

Owl.

The thing they were playing with was an owl.

Just a baby.

The pencil in her mind paused – *oh, the poor little beastie* – but she couldn't stop, because this was good too, the story for her aunt. In fact, it might be better. But what to do now, knowing she would narrate it later back in the house to the Bracebridges. The servants and the view from her window. Her papers and books and desk.

Florence would have to tell the story a different way.

A shout rose from the boy with the red cloth around

his wrist and then he yelled a single word, repeated twice, in Greek. Something that must have meant *go* or *chase* because he led and the others followed a short distance, further from Florence, to where the bird landed on the stones. Florence thought she saw its fear, its defiance, its pain. Her mind picked up the pencil again.

'Stop!' she called, and anybody would have understood, no translation required.

They turned to her and she wondered how she appeared to them. Old? Young? Pretty? Plain? The two boys closest to the owl spoke low and rapidly to each other. Florence caught the words *woman* and *no* and *yes*.

How did she want this part to sound? Florence eyed the owl again and the boy in red. She turned her smile on him – she was twice their age and therefore not at all part of their world. And yet, this would be a rescue story. She would use her charm and sense of justice, her reasoning, which her father had praised in the past.

Swiftly Florence was next to the owl, crouching beside it even though crouching, being small, made her seem weak.

She knew what she was doing; she understood what it meant to persuade these boys to accept her coins, pick up the baby creature, wrap it in her skirt. She knew how it looked, what it meant. By now, all her suitors back in England were married. Other women would have their children. That sort of traditional life (for no more than a moment had she wanted it) was gone.

She cradled the owl and moved her fingers through its downy feathers. Bright eyes stared back.

'Hello to you, too. Would you like to come home with me?'

Dear Aunt Mai …

She knew what it meant to take it back to her apartment in the centre of Athens. To give the bird a name and brook no arguments from her family about how long this pale creature would be with them. For the answer was: as long as it lived, and even beyond that too.

I

South Street, Mayfair
August 1910

Florence

Bodies fall apart. Things come to an end. Everyone wants to make me comfortable, I know that. How many times have I murmured something just the same? *What do you want? What do you need?* What I want though is to feel no pain. What I want is a lover, a swim in the ocean, my body in the grass. What I want is to see. To pick my way through Spitalfields and find the man who used to sell the rabbit, chopped up and gravy-brown in its little bread bed. A bunny bed. Ha. I lick my lips, feel their cracked edges. I rub them together, sending my thoughts to those parts only, till all of me is here, existing in my mouth.

Rory from the village once hallucinated about living there, *in my mouth*. Like I was a great big frog, a gigantic pelican come to take him down the pier – the thrill of being swallowed was very pleasing to a small boy like Rory while he suffered a fever and I nursed him, time and again. He, too, would have aged and now he is who knows where. That sort of mathematics is lost to me. Will it return for my ninety-first birthday? What an unusual gift that would be. Clarity, sense, movement, peace.

Who knew – when I was fourteen and cradling that three-legged blue-grey cat I found; or twenty-one and finding my way through Kew Gardens of an afternoon, dipping a knife into a pot of jam then laying it neatly onto a scone; or thirty-five, watching men die in that kingdom of nightmares – that ninety years would loom up, would bear before me like a terrifying winged thing. That I would be delivered, something useless on the crest of a wave, to face it all alone.

Alone except for one. Mabel, the girl downstairs, who right now is playing a game of drop the pots and pans. Is it a prize to be *my* nurse? Mabel even came from St Thomas's. Just my luck. Who can say if she is the best of the bunch? To me, she first appeared as flat and timid as a stone but has grown to show signs of something rather strong, rather strange.

So.

I am the flotsam and the beach is fast approaching. Mabel is my housekeeper and nurse. I remember the scones from Maids of Honour in Richmond; the jam is made of the finest strawberries grown in France. Did I ever go there?

My brain is trying to get at something and having Mabel tapping about down there isn't helping.

Yes, I may not have all my bits about me, all my wits, but I know where I've been. I was careful once to write it down and I keep that notebook, and all the notebooks, close to me. Writing has been a defence against idleness, against being seen to know nothing. Schoolgirl lessons, letters, records, reports, plans – all a container for my memories. To try to read them now would be a folly. (What did poor unseeing Gloucester say after they took out his eyes? *All dark and comfortless!*) Those notebooks of mine are somewhere in this room. My eyes saw things, my mind worked away at problems, I existed outside this room.

The thing I'm trying to get at: I had a dream last night, a bad dream I've had before. In it, somebody close to me had decided I was to die, with no time to say goodbye to my loved ones. I don't remember the reason – what I had done wrong – but it was distressing to know with certainty that I was facing my final hours on earth, in the company of only my sister and somebody else whose face I didn't recognise. Horrible dream. Sugar? Too much reading before bed? On the mornings after the nightmare – as was the case this morning – I wake up feeling sad and bereft.

So, that's what this is: this niggling sense inside, like a forgotten pet left out in the rain. Here I am, in the late afternoon, finally remembering why I've been feeling peculiar all day, my legs bent beneath my blankets. A glass of bright water sits on my bedside table and my spectacles are in my lap.

I know it is summer. The sun beyond this single-room world of mine is high till eight or nine o'clock. Outside the window a hazel twig reaches towards the glass but misses, shuddering on its long branch. Beneath that, the hideous, rowdy voices from the pub across the street, and automobiles and horses rolling at a clip along the pavement. I used to receive many visitors. But I don't think anybody has been around here for weeks now, months. Instead of wandering off away from home to die in peace, in the way that decrepit dogs do, I have been left all alone by my friends, exactly where I was the last time they saw me. Here to wait for the horrible dream to come again tonight, or for some other terror I don't yet know.

The *lady with the lamp* thing came later, after I returned from the Crimean War, and I could see the appeal. The care with the letter *L*. Its closeness with the word *love*, careful, the tongue in the mouth. To go back there, to when I held that lamp, to be youthful again, to be decisive, to teach and learn and show nothing but strength.

But I have the sense I'm missing something. The sister in my dream was Parthe. The other woman was a nurse I once knew. I recall now the shape of her face, her dark brown hair. A sense of her defiance was baked into my dream – it was not fair that I would die, and this woman felt it too. How peculiar.

When Mabel first arrived at my house she tried all sorts of ways to get me to open up about the war. But what did she expect? The memory wants, sometimes, to forget. A man's head can come clean off his body, like a cork. A man can be frozen inside his greatcoat and must be cut from it like a fish. I was keen to know what Mabel thought the war was about, what she imagined had happened. The Crimea would not have featured in any stories she heard, in any books she read. That part of the continent is so far away. England has never known a night as frigid or water as pitch as that.

It was like this: Mabel was new and she was at the kitchen table trimming beans, which in my whole life I have never done. I was watching her hands go in and out of the bowl. The knife seemed to be part of her and she barely looked at the vegetables, or the blade, or the bowl while she talked. She was twenty-two years old and had come to London from Bournemouth. Her father was a printer and her mother was a seamstress. Mabel was born by the water and lived there as a child. And in her first week in my house she made a joke that because she grew up beside the sea she'd been stuck ever since with water between her ears, which did make me laugh because I'd been thinking to myself, *My dear, you have water between your ears.*

The knife and the beans, the snip of the blade on them and the *pip* sound they made heading back into the bowl drew me to her. She was mesmerising, even as I wondered how this slip of a thing with her curious way of talking would help me navigate the next couple of years, which when you get to eighty-eight – then eighty-nine, then ninety – you assume are your last. When Mabel comes to help me bathe, she inspects me as if it's the first time we've ever met. But she moves the flannel quickly – just like with the beans – and she doesn't linger on any part of me. In fact, it seems she hardly notices my stink and skin and wrinkles and pockets of fat under my arms. What I want most days is a walk in the garden, to feel my feet on the grass. A cup of tea in the evenings, as deep a sleep as I can manage, till I wake in the no-light morning to the sound of horses' hooves on the street. Bed alone, then waking alone to count the seconds and the minutes to *clip-clop clip-clop* till I can rise and ask for Mabel's help again.

Her expectations for me are high. And maybe that's a comfort. *Come on now*, she'll say in her lilting accent. *You did this yesterday, why not now*. Badgering me about eating a mouthful of toast or letting her read to me since my eyesight comes and goes. If I don't motion for her during the day she doesn't seem to mind. She simply goes on chattering away.

Over there. Those same two blue jays are back.

Sure I can't stand those drunkards day in, day out.

My mother left my sister in the middle of the road once, did I tell you that?

All nonsense, though of course I find it soothing. Mothers must speak to their newborns like this. Prattle, prattle, prattle while they're suckling at the breast.

A ring! A bell!

It's coming up from the floor of the earth, calling to me from another realm.

A visitor! I pat down the blankets, turn my head to loosen my neck, wishing I had a lozenge for my mouth.

Another firm knock.

Don't leave.

And now, because it seems clear Mabel isn't going to bother, I finally get up – ninety years old and still having jobs to do! – and walk to the door of my bedroom. The duchess in the corner is open, its tiny drawers jutting out like tongues. How marvellous that suddenly I can see them so clearly. Earlier I'd been searching for an old letter, a particular one, and I'd left all the drawers like that. By morning the duchess will be straightened and the creams and lotions, the hairpins and nets, the dishes containing my brooches, the medals and silver watches, will be in their places. The moonlight lies in stripes across the hardwood floors and across the face of the rug laid in the corner of the room – thick woollen carpet the colour of goose feathers.

The thrill of visitors – that used to happen. Decades ago I would grab my bonnet and slippers and hurry downstairs to meet a gentleman my father had brought home from the village. Or my sister coming up the driveway, arm in arm with a friend she'd collected from the train station. And they would stay in our house for, goodness, days on end. Bold girls that Parthe kept close – the older ones always poking in and out of each room, while I stood back, mouth pursed shut, feeling the bad behaviour like a fog. Such a serious child. So afraid. But that Florence is gone. Gone because I worked that fear out of my system.

Downstairs all is quiet again, but I know the visitor remains. I can sense these things. My body is not the same as other people's – that's for certain. Men liked to say my mind was different – a compliment I recall with fondness. But my hands did the work, my mind made a path, my legs took me halfway round the world. I looked ordinary and goodness knows I haven't checked a mirror for weeks, for months now. But it was my body, my mind, my rules, always.

Use a clear, firm voice so the patient hears you the first time.
Do not ask a patient to turn their head towards you.
Let the light in. Ventilate the room. Clean the utensils.
Change the sheets yourself and do it quickly, without comment.

And so I find I'm able to pull back the bedcovers and set my arthritic feet on the floor and go down the stairs. On the polished hall stand are palm-sized white flowers in a burgundy vase, threads of gold running through it. Who else at ninety is walking down stairs? Or even taking a single step? Who else at ninety is able to remember that we bought the vase from the Assyrian man who used to come by peddling things at Embley even after Mother told him not to?

Parthe used to say it sharply: *If you keep buying his tat, Mother, the man will return.*

I hold the railing and hesitate, one foot in front of the other. If Mabel catches me out here, there'll be trouble. The girl has no qualms about telling me what to do at all hours of the day. Needs to work a little on her manners, needs to work on her gravy, her silence while she prepares food in the kitchen, the dignity in her voice when she asks if I've evacuated my bowels today? This week? Do I require any assistance? There are ways to do it – evacuate a patient's bowels – which all good nurses know. And Mabel's ideas are not those ways. Mabel owns a smart red coat that she throws on when she leaves the house. Very happy to go to the market and to Mr Gong's shop to get the tea. Sometimes it's even part of the same sentence – *Need some help with your bowels, ma'am, I'm on my way to the Chinaman's?* And, oh, the bowels that I myself have seen. I am smiling, my fingers on the balustrade, somehow satisfied with it – the life that, yes, I really did live while I witnessed eye sockets like eggless nests, shattered jaws, the skin on the cheeks of a dehydrated man. Joints and bone and bits of gristle – to think that nobody else ever saw those parts of those poor soldiers, not even their own mothers.

I, too, used to wear a bright coat when I was young. Then later a sash with *Scutari Hospital* stitched across it in blood-red thread.

So: the body I can handle.

This bell, though, these knocks, coming from the front door, are for my mind, and it's that part that's harder to settle now. One foot and then the other.

Who could it be and what could they want?

For a second there's the thought that it's the undertaker, here too soon, and won't he be embarrassed. Ha! Poor Mabel. Could the silly girl have got it so wrong that she's already pronounced me dead and here's the man to shroud me in a sheet and take my bones away? To be buried in Hampshire, no fuss, which I hope they'll respect. I thought she would be a comfort around the house – and occasionally she is, with all that soothing chatter, whether I'm at all interested in what she has to say or not. There was something else, too, that meant I was drawn to her and not the other girl they sent over – almost exactly one year ago. Mabel chews the ends of her hair when she thinks I'm not watching and always has something, some lozenge or comfit, that she runs through her mouth like water. And so here we are together, and I hope she does not think I have died. No!

A noise like a honk comes from my mouth, and I un-drown myself awake. I realise it was yet another dream, and the honk was my attempt at that forceful *No!* To lose language while we sleep has always felt degrading.

So I didn't walk down the stairs.

I smooth the blanket, stare at the glass of water.

A fool to think it. I try to roll my ankles beneath the blanket. A pain nestles in my bladder. And, still, the aftersound of the knock at my door hangs in the air.

Silas

The distance from the corner to her house can't be more than fifty, sixty paces, but I'm sure I left the corner after midday and by the time I lean over to unlatch her gate the quarter-moon is sharp and vivid in the night sky. The stars have slid out as if from under paper. It's all very different for me, you see. Time. And distance and space and my body in it. And something else that's different for me: the night sky, because of how many times I've seen it. More times than that man over there checking his pocket watch, unaware that a pigeon is hovering above his head. More times than that man who is pushing back his green cap to wipe at his forehead with a handkerchief.

I have a knack for directions, ever since the war, ever since my time in the Crimea, in France, in Brighton. Miss

Nightingale's house has black-trimmed windows and globes of light pocketed beside the front door, a handsome house in busy Mayfair. It is draped in trees and the air is drummed with the sounds of horses' hooves and a swing of music coming from a nearby hotel. I'm good at directions, yes, but it's taken me years to get here. And now that I'm here, moving up towards her front door, I'm unable to speak. For a time, I watch the electricity surge through the lights inside and outside the house. And what a marvel it is to witness. Nothing less than magic, like blood through a bloodstream.

The door.

I am silent.

I whisper into the evening air a thank-you to the woman at St Thomas's in Lambeth. I had circled the courtyard (hard to believe that was today) of the vast hospital, aware that I might be attracting attention that I didn't want. Around and around. Till eventually I entered one of the pavilions and spied a senior-looking uniformed woman who I stopped to ask if she knew where I might find Miss Nightingale. I thought the nurse might believe I was the grandson of a soldier from the Crimea. *Flowers* – I raised my voice over the din of a bell going off behind me – I wanted to leave flowers outside Miss Nightingale's gate in memory of my grandfather.

'You mean to get there on foot?' the ward sister asked.

I could not tell from her tone what the correct answer was. She wrote something on a square of paper but didn't give it to me. She regarded me while around us the hospital churned efficiently and quietly.

With some difficulty I raised a hand and motioned towards the river. 'It's a beautiful day,' I said, which could mean anything, either yes or no. And it seemed she approved, making a few more strokes with her pencil.

'A beautiful day,' she repeated. 'And not too far.' She smoothed the paper map in her palm.

Now I raise a fist to the door on Mayfair and knock. And after that, when there is no answer, I ring the bell. A moment later, it opens.

'Hello,' I say.

'Hello, sir.'

Standing on the front steps is a young woman with chestnut hair, cut short under a bonnet, and dark, shining eyes. She wears a sort of maid's dress of thin green stripes that has buttons to the neck and a square pocket on her left breast. Is it ash on her white apron? Food from the kitchen? She has a delicate face, a nose that is slightly too large for it. Above her, a light is turned on in its copper holder.

'Sir?'

I realise time is passing unnaturally. I try again: 'Good evening.'

'Good evening,' she replies.

My chest swells. 'Hello,' I say.

She cocks her head to the side. A tiny smile is on her lips. 'Sir, is there something else?'

'Yes, of course.'

'What can I do for you?'

'Does Florence Nightingale live here?'

'Miss Nightingale?' Her face seems to close up. My eyes are drawn to that pocket on her dress – it's as though she herself is a small treasure and is tucking herself within it.

I point towards Green Park. 'I've just now walked from Lambeth. From the hospital.'

'The hospital sent you?'

'No, miss, that's not quite it. I knew Miss Nightingale. Years ago.'

'Sir? I—'

'Silas Bradley.' I tap myself on the chest then point up. 'These are a marvel, aren't they? The lights. Electricity?'

I catch a scar like a carpenter's notch on the underside of her chin.

'I rather like them myself, Mr Bradley, and I do think they're a marvel. Did you come to talk about any other parts of the house?'

I shake my head. 'Forgive me. And what is your name?'

No hesitation but now she's taken a pair of scissors from her pocket and is snipping off a white flower from a bush beside the steps. She pockets it. 'It's Miss Watt. Mabel Watt.'

'Like Mr Watt?'

'Pardon me?'

'You're famous then. Your forebear invented the steam engine. And here we are talking about electricity.'

She narrows her eyes. 'I'm afraid I don't know who it is you're talking about or even if you're making fun of me.'

'Oh.' In my other life my face and neck would be red with a surge of blood. I raise a hand to my temple. 'I'm sorry,' I said. 'Not making fun, no.'

'Are you selling something?'

'No,' I say, 'that isn't it.' I lean forward, careful not to touch her arm. Resisting even though I want to, strangely, badly.

'You mentioned my mistress, Miss Nightingale.'

'Yes, we knew each other in the Crimea, in Turkey, at Scutari.' It isn't a breath I take – I no longer do that. But I expand my chest, *in-out*. I pause. 'I'm wondering if I might see her.'

Mabel Watt smiles but seems confused. 'She is not well – perhaps you don't know this.'

'I know,' I say. 'Or, rather, I assumed as much. She doesn't have long.'

Mine is not a question and Mabel doesn't try to argue. She gazes at me, the blades of the scissors pointing down to her boots. She is prepared to use them on me. This thought has occurred to her at this exact moment. A switch turned on.

'If,' I say, 'I could be permitted just one moment with Miss Nightingale, I think it would help us both at this late stage.'

'Help you?'

'But mostly her. She is restless up there, without peace.'

I feel her breath go in and out. No matter if she notices something unusual about me, how there is no breath of mine to match hers. The white flowers against their dark leaves glow. Above us the twin lights gleam. I follow her eyes up. The tiring part, for me, is over. I wait.

Finally, she asks, 'You were friends?'

I allow myself to reach out and pat her soft arm, the one holding the scissors. 'That's it. At Scutari. Friends.'

Florence

The wind is pelting the trees and the branches are frightening themselves. Will I ever leave this house again with my eyes open? I've helped deliver babies who were born with open eyes, their bodies seeming to spin in my hands. I blink to make the memory stay, to keep the fear out. But the memory snaps shut and the wind beats at the window again and again.

All those years when I had demands placed on my time – they are gone forever. Mothers and fathers own their unwed daughters, pressing and shaping them till they marry, and then they are finished. The daughter who doesn't marry is peculiar. Mother didn't know what to do with me and neither did Parthe, who acted like Mother's agent. I couldn't be fathomed. What would I do if I wasn't a wife? Even if I married, which I thought about doing several times – then what? Perhaps no man would have known how to fathom me either.

From Germany, I wrote back home – here! I found it! Educated women of England, I will give you something to do and no vows to take! Nursing could be a noble, disciplined and practical endeavour. The nurses of Kaiserswerth – and many of them were peasants – were pure love. I wasn't a mystery to them. What I sought to do was natural.

It all sounded marvellous but I hadn't told my family what I was doing or where I was going in Germany. Of course they discovered I'd sneaked off and of course they hounded me. Parthe threw herself about, took ill, and didn't speak to me for months. Mother and Father were mortified, furious, afraid I would leave them. All I could do was keep the memory of that light-filled place in Düsseldorf deep inside. When they chastised me I had only to think about it to feel invigorated, right there at the dining table with the lace and linen all around me, the flowers in vases. Of course I felt guilty! This was all my doing, their vexation with me. I was a second daughter instead of a son, a baby born in Italy, coming into their lives to disturb their peace. I crashed through their drawing room. People confected the fabulous story that leaving my family and our wealth to go to the Crimea was a sacrifice – it was no such thing. It was a lifeline. God's will, His voice in my head. I had dreamt of being heroic, which women never are. I dreamt of being useful.

Mabel knocks but doesn't come through.

'Are you a daughter?' I say to the empty room.

She opens the door. 'Pardon, ma'am?'

'You are a daughter? You have a mother and a father?'

It is not a difficult question and yet Mabel speaks slowly. 'Yes, ma'am. I have a mother and a father.'

My mouth has dried up again. This is all I can manage most days.

'Ma'am, did you hear the bell? A young man is here.'

'Oh.' The visitor!

'He says he knows you from Scutari.'

A shudder passes across my chest. It's been years since Scutari so how could I know a young man? Not a *young man*. Surely it's Mabel, excited, rushing, getting the message wrong. She is forever bumping into side tables, absent-minded girl, mussing her fingers across panes of glass. Body, heart, mind, her extremities – all the parts of a clock marginally out of time.

'Scutari, ma'am,' she repeats.

But then I recall those other soldiers who have found me here on South Street in the dead of night, although those ones came through the walls or down from the ceiling, landing on my bed like cats. At Scutari I'd called them my children, so it seemed only fair they would come to find me in my old age – but this time by the front door!

When I was a young woman I kept an owl as a pet. More than once in my life I felt the ghost of that bird visiting me at night to burble in my ear and pedal her claws across my legs. It seemed that the owl – Athena was her name – needed to wake me with this fact: *thousands of men died at my hospital in Scutari.*

Dread then to have to face this again tonight. But inexorable – however they arrive, they will be let in.

'How many?' I ask. Mabel is hard to make out beside my bed, my eyes almost useless.

'Pardon, ma'am?'

'How many men?'

'One.'

I nod at Mabel, hoping she understands. *Yes, bring him in.*

And fear now at who this man is and what his true purpose might be. I shuffle across the bed and pull a cloth from my drawer. I mean to pat my cheeks with it but I sit against the headboard and twist the flannel between my fingers. In distress, my mind often goes to my sister. A memory: Parthe cornering me in the carriage on the way to East Wellow, covering my eyes. *How do you always know when things are about to happen?* I didn't know what she meant. *Yes, you do. You see things when there's nothing real to see.*

I hear Mabel's muffled voice on the landing, but she doesn't come back in. Instead a different figure slips through the doorway and I feel him before I see him. And this figure coming, me lifting my eyes to him across the length of my bed, makes me think that, yes, perhaps Parthe in the carriage was correct. Her voice hot in my ear, a posy of flowers in my lap.

The man has pain in his joints, he feels the cold, time is rushing past him in odd and confounding ways. I sense his fear like a pup.

I ache all over and the man looks upon me as though he knows.

'Miss Nightingale,' he says. But I will not be *Miss Nightingale* for much longer. I am being tugged away.

'You're one of them, aren't you?' I ask. 'Come closer.'

An icy breeze, and a transmission of the man's pain, his pleading fear – it drifts towards me.

'You've travelled a long way. Tell me, what is your name?'

'Silas Bradley.'

But of course I already know.

With the effort coming off me in waves, I rise further up the bed and pull my wrapper tight. I don't need to explain that I haven't had visitors in years. I glance at the room. Not just an old lady but a bereft and lonely one.

'How did you find me?' I ask.

'They told me at St Thomas's.' His eyes are fixed on me and I try to do the same in return.

'I haven't been there in years.' Can he see my mind picturing the hospital on the riverbank, the bright pavilions I helped to design, the nurses moving inside?

'It's an impressive place,' he says. 'Enormous.'

'And where did you grow up, Silas? You, as a boy: this was a long time ago, wasn't it?'

'In Buckinghamshire, ma'am.'

That iciness again. It is him, it is him. He is here. He is here and I am running out of air. The windows in the barracks are too low, too airless. I cannot breathe. A window, a window.

I float my hands to my heart. The next question needs to be asked, but I can barely speak it. 'Do you mean to take me away?'

Silas

The question throws me. I shake my head slowly, till she is doing the same and is in unison with me.

'No,' I say.

'No,' she repeats. She doesn't let go of her chest.

I had expected her to be fragile and meek or with no memory of me and who I might be. Or even of Scutari itself.

Instead, when Mabel brought me to her, Miss Nightingale sat up straighter. She adjusted herself and when I came through the door she said, 'Oh.'

I took her silence for needing me to fill it – like me, perhaps she cannot abide silence – and when I spoke again, she replied, simply, 'It's you.'

And all I could think to say was, 'Yes. It's me.'

She motioned – entirely delicate while also being forceful,

sharp, this woman with her elegant hand; she would brook no arguing.

'Come. Sit.'

A burst of pain rode the side of my body and held me captive for a few seconds. Could she tell? I paused before setting off across the rug on the floor. I urged myself to move smoothly, her gaze on me, acute beneath the fringe of her lace bonnet.

'Do you know who I am?' I finally asked.

'I know where you've come from,' she said. 'I know you're here to remind me of things.'

I nodded, though my brain was foggy and the pain was deep and radial from my side, the site where my death first occurred.

'Yes,' I said. 'Her name was Jean Frawley. At this late hour we both need to know what happened.'

'Miss Frawley.'

'Oh.' It escaped my mouth. 'You do remember.'

'I never forgave myself.'

Her mind was at work; I could almost see the flickering images that jagged and snagged inside.

'It is right to be haunted,' she said. 'It is right that you have haunted me.'

'Ma'am, it isn't haunting I'm for. I simply need— What did Jean do to me?'

And that was when she asked her question. *Do you mean to take me away?*

That afternoon in Marseilles, my head spun with freedom and the rawness I felt being among people wearing warm clothes and taking cups of coffee in a dainty restaurant. In that restaurant, I first saw Jean and all the breath seemed to leave my body. *Ah!* I thought. *Here's a soul like mine, a soul who doesn't quite fit.*

Now I stand above Miss Nightingale – she is a floating head above a sea of tight blankets. She wears black silk, lacy and soft yet somehow regal on the bed. The room seems to live in her.

She reaches for a glass of water and I notice the way her fingers do not tremble and her gaze takes me in – all of me, and I crumble a little from it. I remember adults staring when I was a child and I hated it. Adults who seemed to know more about me and my family than I cared to share. For a brief moment all feeling comes back to me, spilling its way through my limbs and skin with a flash of vigour. To be seen. To be believed.

'I know ghosts,' she says. 'My dear pet, for example.'

She picks at the blanket edge closest to her, which is white with fine tassel threads. I imagine her with a puppy, or a fat snowy cat. But she reveals that the pet was an owl she rescued and loved, a naughty thing. I picture a gilded cage, its talons gripping the silky fabric of a rich lady's arm.

'I saw her,' she tells me. 'Long dead now. Her name was Athena. She was perched on the edge of the cliffs at Scutari. The city of Constantinople – do you remember it? The view from the barracks? The sea was like tin. The sky was a veil over all those stars. I had walked past the hospital and I was surely tired but I know what I saw. It was Athena and she came so close. As if she sought me out, but, having found me, was content to bob her head a few times, bowing. And off she went, down over the cliff and away.'

Stirred by her words, stirred by her memory, recognising she had kept it hidden or even forgotten, I find myself close to tears recalling the Barrack Hospital, across the water from Constantinople. And now we're in our own fading worlds: me thinking about Jean Frawley, and the great Miss Nightingale alone in a strange land with her beloved pet summoned late one night.

Florence

I am five or six years old again, with a high pale forehead and pale eyebrows – two facts that even at a young age are starting to occur to me, starting to irritate me. My sister's eyebrows are painterly, thick brown flecks above her eyes. Parthe is very pretty, older than me by one year. We are home, this time at Lea Hurst, and my mother is brushing my hair. She has me sitting on a tall stool in the doorway to the back garden, boxes and boots and a pile of dirt-covered pumpkins in a basket at my feet. She puts the brush down on a white towel, then picks up her pair of silver scissors. The breeze is tearing up the hairs on my arm, the hairs on my head, and the sun is diving in and out of view as I open and shut my eyes. I feel the scissors as a single blade across the skin above my eyes, and it's as though they're writing a word up there.

On a stone wall outside in the sunshine, Parthe sits perched like a velvety cat. Finally she rises on her long legs, jumps, lands lightly on her feet.

Then there's the sound that I'll always associate with scissors, which at that very moment pierce – just slightly – my forehead. Through a veil of my hair, my mother is saying, 'Oh, Florence! Oh, dear!'

But it's a gun making the noise, and I've heard gunshots countless times. Men come to shoot in the fields by our house, and Parthe and I are allowed to watch from the front porch.

Parthe approaches to inspect the blood. 'Did you do that?' she asks our mother.

Mother snips the scissors together and they make their silky sound. 'I did.'

'By accident,' I say.

All three of us touch our fingers to the spot and they come away with flecks of blood.

Parthe says, 'It's good you're getting a fringe to hide it.'

Another gunshot and then the muffled, baggy cry of a grouse before it thuds to the ground. Mother snips off one last feather of hair. 'There. I told you today would be a good day for it.'

She turns around and slides the scissors cleanly between the wings of the towel. That is her job done for the day. We don't know much about what else she does, being a mother. She talks to the staff a lot, especially the cook. Parthe and

I have witnessed Mother fill vases, brush her hair, shake out books then put them back in their shelves, tuck blankets around her toes while she reads, go for walks and carriage rides, herd the house's kittens into their basket, dip her little finger into cups of tea when she thinks nobody is watching. She is forever being interrupted.

Parthe grabs my hand and we head towards the sound of the shot. My new hair across my forehead makes me feel sharper, like I can see new things. We tramp down the long grass and past the ducks that are ours and the other ducks that are just ducks, not belonging to anybody. It is late summer, and the warm green grass is alive with millions of insects. Pollen and dust glint in the air. Parthe and Mother are often on the hunt for flowers for pressing, for nature to reveal a new colour that they might buy, as silky thread, in London.

The lawn at the back of the house yawns out towards the river, which is slow and brown, and swallows things whole. I hear the hum of water and the wind taking slices out of the air.

Once, I found a hare, injured in the grass. I was by myself so I folded it into my skirt, blood everywhere, and carried it inside. I tipped out my dolls and laid the hare in their box. I wrapped a bandage around its paw, up and down, to stop the flow of blood. Thank God I was there to save it.

When I come here alone, He knocks gently on my ears and I let His words flow through me like water.

Sun, daughter, mother, sky.

Goodness, kindness, rest.

Standing above me, Parthe asks, 'Have you ever seen God?'

I say nothing.

She tries again. 'What are you really praying for at night?'

'I haven't ever seen God,' I tell her, because I know she doesn't mean: *Have you seen God reflected in the river, or in the family of baby frogmouths that appeared in the yard one day, or in our pegged-up nightdresses flapping in the breeze?* Because of course I've seen God in those ways.

'What do you think He looks like?'

'Like a nice man you might run into in the village,' I say. 'He has a beard. His eyes are dark and shiny and He is tall, taller than Papa.'

Parthe drops next to me and kicks out her feet, scattering blades of grass from her fists. 'And at night? Before bed?'

I toss my new hair and turn back to the house. 'I pray that I will do good things. I say sorry for the things I've done wrong.'

Parthe leans over and presses her thumb to the cut on my forehead. She smiles, and I choose to think it's because she sees me as wise and strong. *God is everywhere*, I think, but do not say. *God is even in the wound.*

———

The soldier. He is handsome, rather short, rather sad. Dark brown hair and black-ish eyes. A youthful face and cheeks, solid features but a slight air. A man who resembles a boy.

I've always been good at details. Nurses owe it to their patients to seek out their faces and find them properly, even briefly, to look each one in the eye. (The rest of their blown-up, starved, caved-in, bloodied, infested bodies are images that have endlessly sought me out. A recollection of a different soldier presses on me now, his leg that needed removing. He was one of surgeon Calloway's patients, and therefore no anaesthetic was offered, and he was dead two hours later. I cannot remember the face of that poor soul.)

But this soldier.

'I would remember you even if you weren't beside me right now,' I tell him.

He glances away, nervously, it seems.

'Do you believe me?' I ask.

'You don't have to say you remember me, ma'am.'

'Is your mind my mind?'

'No, ma'am.'

'Again, what is your name?'

'It's Silas.'

He says it as though he prizes it, this word.

I repeat: 'Silas.' I get: flash of briny seawater, flash of pearl-handled spoon, flash of rib cage open to the air.

And then I get: brown hair, pretty girl, poor girl, girl who had never been anywhere, never been to a place like the café in

Marseilles. I get: strange girl who liked to watch the surgeons work, the same way I did.

Jean. The woman in my dream last night.

'Please don't fuss over the recalling,' Silas says. 'There were thousands of us.'

'Thousands. Yes.' I am suddenly tired, light-headed. Have never felt so light-headed. Have I eaten? Have I drunk today? Surely Mabel has taken care of all that.

Silas says, 'But only one of me. Like this. Turning up at your door fifty-five years on. Would that be right?'

I manage to shake my head. What *is* this man?

After my time in the Crimea, McNeill tried to convince me there was nothing I could have done to prevent the vast numbers of deaths. That I did my best to save the lives of all those souls. But why shouldn't I remember them and their eyes and mouths, or the way some, like Silas, had hair curling round their ears, leaving you to believe they'd been that way since they were mere boys? McNeill's words, when I could recall them, let me think for a time that I was blameless. Is there anything better in this world? But in other moments my guilt ran away with his comments, like a tide washing back out to the ocean.

I am drawn to a flutter at my window that brings her to mind: Athena. My beloved owl who loved shiny things and who slept in my lap like a cat. Who had I told, all these years, about her visits to me, long after she was gone? That I still see her? Athena the ghost, or the dream of a ghost.

The man is keen to find my eye, to drag it back from the window. He's shuffled closer to my bed.

'So have there been others from Scutari?' he asks.

I spot a tuft of cotton thread on my blanket and pinch at it once, twice, to pluck it off. It is hard for me to watch his sadness. A look of almost humiliation comes over his face. He seems like the loneliest man in the world.

'Yes,' I say. Now he'll want to know who's come before.

'How many?'

'Plenty,' I reply. 'Enough.'

Sometimes they come through the window, sometimes from behind the mirror. They never stay long.

'But never through the front door,' I add. 'That's new.'

Imagine if my family were here to see my life flooded with soldiers. My mother, my sometimes-darling mother, long gone now and not one for fanciful things, would have driven them from the house herself, and off into the night. She could never stomach things the way others could. Was it that simple? Her constitution? She showed me love but I saw how her body thrummed with everything she was suppressing in each moment, never saying so.

'I've had no real visitors, not for months, I think. You seem different from the rest.'

The colours in my room swirl together and a fog descends across my eyes.

At times, I comfort those boys in my dreams – sometimes they let me. My children. I wipe their brows, saying things will be better soon. But if I touch them for too long it hurts them and, before I wake, they're in pain again. I gather them close, and in my dreams my tears catch fire.

Silas

And now Miss Nightingale is mewling, fussing against her pillows. I've upset her.

'Please, ma'am, forgive me. I'm sorry – I needed to come.'

The girl Mabel enters the room. She takes my hand in her warm one and fixes me with a firm expression.

'Come, let her rest.'

Before we go, Miss Nightingale calls out, 'Mabel, keep him with you.'

The girl leads me downstairs, then along a passageway past a cabinet of bowls and plates. We emerge into the kitchen. Mabel invites me to sit at one end of the yellow wooden table. The cupboards are painted light green. A porcelain sink on narrow legs is fixed against one wall. On the table are pitchers and glasses, bowls and cloths. Through a high window, glassy cold, is the moon, though the sky is still light. To think I was outside for so long studying this house. Perhaps I saw that exact window, my teeth chattering and the ropy pain going up and down my limbs.

Mabel fills the kettle and sets it on the stove. With a flick the gas is on. 'She doesn't talk much anymore, you know.'

'I felt she had a bit to say.'

'I talk enough for both of us.'

'Will she let me up again, do you think?'

'She might. You cannot change her mind. If she's thinking, *I won't say another word*, then you can rely on that.'

I study the square tiles on the floor – brown, white and black. So: Miss Nightingale may not speak again. It will be all my questions and nothing from her. Fine.

'But really,' Mabel says, leaning across the bench, 'where are you from?'

'Today?'

'Before today.'

'I've been in London for some time now. Before that: Buckinghamshire. Before that: far away in Europe.'

'So you've come all that way. You've known her for that long?' She blows a strand of hair away from her lips and tucks it under her white cap. 'How many years?'

'I can't remember. I mean: I don't keep score. I can't.'

She nods at this. Probably thinks I'm barmy, which is fine. Lovely girl, beautiful strange face. Happy mouth even when she isn't talking.

Happy mouth. Words that make me think: *happy mother.*

Flash of being back in our kitchen when I was a child and tiptoeing down the hallway so as not to wake her, my mother. Who never yelled at me, not once. But sleep was what she needed.

Mabel might mind me in her kitchen, but she doesn't show it. I can sense that of all the places in this vast and warm house, Mabel feels most at ease in this room. I ask about her family, and how she ended up here. She makes tea and it offers me comfort, the warmth of the cup drawing away some of the pain in my fingers for a time.

'Where is your family from?'

'Bournemouth,' she says. 'Do you know it?'

'Never known anybody from there,' I say. 'Do you like the sea?'

'Oh, very much. I was always a girl up to my knees or my neck in the sea with my dog beside me – we had lots of dogs over the years. We'd be leaping about in the water. The children from the neighbourhood, all of us together.'

I tell her it sounds beautiful. That she must feel lucky, that she might wish she lived there still. Mabel is emptying a pot of water, and when she pauses, the water seems to stop in a wave, mid-air over the basin, like magic. I glance at her to see if she notices too.

'I suppose it was. Beautiful, I mean. London is hard. The people here are not as friendly. I miss my father and mother.'

'Are they …?'

'Yes. Still alive, both my parents.' She resumes her work at the basin and I watch the water spill out cleanly. 'He was a printer. My mother is a seamstress; she's younger than my father by about ten years. She's always been good at fixing things. People in town, sometimes strangers, will come to her for help – clothes, bodies, no matter.'

A vision of lively Mabel and her family as makers and fixers sits comfortably with me. She picks up carrots, turnips, a brush to scrub them with.

In a whisper she says, 'I've taken Miss Nightingale on trips to visit a healer. Not recently, but once or twice before.'

'Could they help? Was she willing to go?'

'Well, not a lot can be done. It was mostly about keeping her comfortable. And the people recognised her! She was not above being helped, but when I returned home with her the last time, she told me that was enough and it was time to stay. She would pray and wait and rest. It now seems something like a sign, like a trial.'

I think: *A trial for whom?*

As if reading my mind, Mabel says, 'A bit like penance.'

She slices the turnips into fine discs, and sets a fresh pot of water on the cookstove.

She lowers her voice again and says, 'She's ninety. I've never known anybody that old.'

'Neither have I.' And I think of all the men dead in the Crimea at no more than a quarter of her age. Had they lived – and I count myself among these imaginings – those men might be fathers and grandfathers now. And I am twenty-seven but I am also eighty-three. I have no children. I've lived two lives and yet a full life has quite escaped me. I remember the Crimea, ships arriving on the coal-black sea. Steam and smoke rose from their decks and I saw their huge lumbering bodies as though we were part of a game being played invisibly from above. Our rations: one-and-a-half pounds of bread (brown) and one pound of meat (foul) per day. I would lift myself onto one elbow and try to wrap my blanket better around me. No point thinking about apples or cake or pie or biscuits (the French had biscuits). Instead, why not think I was a thousandth my size. All that food! Those seeming pounds of bread and heaping serves of brown meat. I could never hope to finish it all. That was how I endured that bit, you see. Tricking myself, in control.

'Did it work?'

So I'd said those things aloud and Mabel was listening. She turns in the space between the larder and the bench where I sit with my tea.

'Well,' I say, 'I don't often feel hungry now. I've forgotten the taste of that bread. Must have worked.'

We are sitting in the almost-night together. Mabel has a cloth in her pocket and a lozenge in her mouth that clacks against her teeth when she talks. All these years I've watched women's hairstyles changing but I've not seen anything like Mabel's, cropped and barely longer than a man's.

'Can you eat?' she asks. 'Now?'

'Very small amounts. Like a baby bird.'

'Do you sleep?'

'I love to sleep. More and more as time goes on.'

'And all the people around you in the city – they're moving past to sit on a train or take a table at the pub? They can see and hear and touch you?'

'Yes, yes. Just like anybody, I suppose.'

From 1880 to the turn of the century, or thereabouts, I was sensitive to the cold. That's why I travelled south. But for the past ten years it's the heat that gets to me. Summertime now and the streets of London – I can feel them through my boots. Hot bricks. Scalding stones that I pick up and drop into the pond in the park. The sun against my skin. Of course I take off what clothing I can, what is permissible for a man in a park during daylight hours to remove. It wouldn't do for me to get arrested and, thankfully, I never have been.

In the kitchen with this young woman (the clacking in the mouth; the mud-brown eyes; her fingers kind of lazy and loose, trailing over objects in a way that makes you think she's dropped something important every day of her life), I observe the way she is unimpressed with me, even as she is curious about my life and body and what has brought me here. A woman like this is what Miss Nightingale has decided she needs in her final hours. I can see it; yes, Mabel's simplicity and mildness would dispatch me quite nicely into the night.

Pain shoots from one side of my chest to the other. I am soft bread that somebody is tearing into. A seam opens through me. I lied when I told Mabel I don't keep count. I do. I can read and I know the numbers. It isn't fair for a man to wait this long, to wonder what he did wrong. Where it all went wrong.

'What's happening?' Mabel asks. 'Are you cold? Would you like a blanket?'

'I think so,' I say, fatigue coming over me like a caul. I picture myself tucked up beside Mabel; her sweetly scented hair would send me to sleep. She leaves the room and it feels emptied of warmth while I sit alone at the yellow table with its dishes and scales. The water isn't yet boiling and the kitchen's coldness creeps up from the soles of my feet to my very insides.

'Mabel?'

And then she is back in the doorway with a blanket over one arm. 'Will this be enough?'

'Thank you,' I say.

'Shall I take you to the drawing room? You can lie down.'

But I don't want to be without her and I don't know what might creep out of the walls at me. I tell her I will stay in the kitchen. I take the blanket and wrap it around my shoulders.

She sets about slicing again, shifts to the pot and rests her hand, clad in a cloth, against its sides to test it.

One thought: *Keep talking*. For silence terrifies me nearly as much as wondering what the night will bring when I am eventually turfed out of here and into the street.

I ask, 'Can I tell you a story? It's about a healer too.'

Bayswater, the summer of 1872. I fold my arms across my body as I edge into Hyde Park, past a child in a dress with a nanny standing solidly nearby, and a pair of black dogs going wild for their owner, a man taunting them playfully with a brown paper package held above his head. I bend to go under a tree branch rather than around it. Energy is low today. Feeling lost and tired, I need to curl up somewhere. Something catches my attention beyond a stand of trees. It's a hare, precisely like the one I saw when I was a boy. It might well be the same one, slipping through time. Time is a river; time is a long green grassy bank. Why couldn't it be the same animal, here again to rock on its paws at the sight of me?

The pain in my side is back to haunt me. My chest is taking on gusts of wind, leaving me feeling as though I'm a whistling pipe. Deep *in-out*, *in-out* and hope I can work the aches out. I'm ill with longing for my old house and those meadows. A sickness often seems to draw me back to the home of my childhood, even when it is hard to get there. A longing too for Marseilles and Jean: her prettiness, her warmth, that great and wild look in her eyes.

Near the Serpentine I hope to meet a woman I've heard can cure the pain in the soles of my feet. At night, asleep in the boarding house near Hampstead Heath, I feel a taut pulling along the skin. Not an itch, although I have been known to scratch my fingers along my soles for what seems like hours. It's more of a throbbing, a stretching. Glass in my feet? Hundreds of shards that nobody can find? A pain that simply will not go away.

I take a moment to breathe in the fertile air. I feel the pastures – tumbling, messy, rambling lawns – like a thread of colour down my nose and throat and into my lungs. My father once told me that Hyde Park began as a hunting ground for a king. I note many places where an injured pheasant could seek shelter from dogs lacing across the grass with their noses to the ground, following invisible lines over neat green hills. Gunshots would have rung out. I let a shiver pass through my body. Summer brings with it a range of scents and tastes on the tip of my tongue that I find impossible to ignore.

The woman's name is Enid. I saw a poster tacked to a pole in Spitalfields, proclaiming her ability to treat ailments such as mine, and I want it to be true, for God knows I have tried in the past and got nowhere. The house in Hampstead lets the light in, which my body needs in summer. Four of us live there – three other men and me – but I miss the warmth of a woman beside me. As I lift my legs high to cross a particularly overgrown stretch of pasture, I think about my near-empty bedroom and the hollow sounds that the other men make. Some days I can barely remember their names. One is an articled clerk, one is a coachman and one is a poet who never seems to sleep. If we run into one another outside our rooms, we're quick to turn away and hurry off. Summer, 1872, and I more closely resemble the man I was at twenty. Who knows what my housemates think of me? After I untacked the poster from the pole, I took it home and set it on my dresser. It said that Enid sells her remedies at the Serpentine on Fridays from noon.

The thought of relief from the relentless pain in my feet – as I swish through the grass and look up when a man yells *Kite!* and a glorious black and red kite swirls against the blue – makes my joints tingle as well. *Enid*, I think. *Save me.*

In the distance I spy her stall, a white tent held up high in the middle and a poster hung from the front flap: *Salves, remedies and comfits sold here.* A gardener throws a clump near my feet that seems so alive I think it's a dirty bird. I jump back – but it's just a ball of earth with its roots like entrails. The gardener grunts and tosses another one, this time to his other side. I let a swallow switch direction thrice in front of me, careful not to trip over it, marvelling at its indecision, its all-the-time-in-the-world beadiness. Can it see me for what I am? The Serpentine eddies beside me, cradling its current, sieving through it.

The sun was high in the sky when I arrived at Hyde Park. I wonder if it takes me minutes or hours to cross the grass as I notice how the sun has slid down. When I make it to

Enid's tent I feel something new in the air. All the sounds – the swallows' birdsong, shouts from the gardeners poaching the weeds from the overgrown bed – are closing in on me. I must concentrate. I am here to find a remedy.

At the tent, I wait. No other patient comes out. Then a figure emerges in a burgundy dress and apron.

'Are you Enid?' I ask.

'I am. You're here to see me?'

'I have pains in my joints that are getting worse and I need help.' I feel tears in my eyes as I say these words.

'Quick then. This way.'

A hard wooden chair with my arms outstretched. Enid finally stops her pacing and unfurls her fingers and traces – something – up and down my neck. At first, I feel nothing. Then a thrill, a tickle, and I recall the desire I had to remain alive right before the whole river rushed into my chest.

'How old are you?'

'I'm forty-five.'

Enid's fingers lift from my skin. She holds her breath for a few seconds and I drop my eyes. Then her thumbs are back on my forearms, this time rubbing, trying to get at something, which of course I have been trying to do as well.

'Forty-five,' she repeats.

It's difficult to reply. 'Thereabouts.'

Enid's chest rises.

'We live in unusual times, don't we?' she muses. 'Multiple lives inside us always, sinking or wrestling for our attention, giving us joy or pain – do you believe that? It isn't only one life. I'm here now, but I'm also somewhere else.' She cocks her head to one side. 'I'm also on a long, low boat in the canal. I am six years old, maybe I am seven, and I've just seen a duck bob into the water from the edge of the canal and grab out a fish! But all the while I am here with *you*. Can you see? Both.'

'Yes.'

'Do you feel that too?'

'Sometimes. Yes.'

Enid is short and seems to glide around the tent. At a table with long legs she untwists lids, dipping a finger into the substances inside. Outside, the noises from the day start up again. They reach my ears and I grow weary thinking of trudging home through crowds and across streets, hoping I don't forget my way or get asked by a beggar for a coin or tobacco.

'And have you always felt it?' Soon she approaches me, circling two fingers through something in her left palm.

'I think I have,' I say. 'But when I was young, I didn't recognise that's what it was.' Relief at talking about it, and no shame in the oddness. All those hours at church as a boy being told I had half a brain in my head – it was because I was *elsewhere*.

What comes out of Enid's palm is the colour of pig fat, cold and creamy when she smooths it onto my wrists. She feeds some of it into an empty jar and shows me how much to put on my feet and ankles (here she bends down and lifts the leg of my trousers). She writes on a scrap of paper, folds it. I take it, pay her, thank her, and leave feeling dizzy and shattered by exhaustion. A fizzing settles in my limbs, as if bugs are in my veins. But this time: not unpleasant.

I take a shortcut east. In winter, I saw skaters gather on the ice holding torches and gliding in formations across the frozen surface. Fathers, mothers, children wrapped up. But today the moon is garlanded and blurry against the closing of the day. The gauzy sweet light of summer is over everything, and the sun not quite gone by ten o'clock. Children are playing at the water's edge, producing sticks from their hands to toss in. Boundless energy.

Could I make it to Jean's old address? I pat the jar in my pocket. Maybe this is the hour, pain-free, when I finally track her down.

'Jean?' Mabel says from across the table. 'Who's that?'

'Miss Nightingale and I knew her years ago.'

'And did you go to her house?'

'Many times.'

'Did you find her?'

'No, never. Has Miss Nightingale … Perhaps Miss Frawley has visited?'

'Here? I don't think so.'

I undo the blanket and bundle it into my lap.

Mabel studies my face then changes her tone: 'But perhaps she did! Before my time. It's possible.'

Florence

I hear Mabel closing a door loudly downstairs. Is the man with her in my kitchen? Hard now to recall him – eyesight failing, my memory full of holes. Socks on his feet, grey trousers, pressed shirt, dark vest? His brown hair, yes, just as I remember, curling around his ears.

I recall once more the girl Jean who wanted to hold a dead man, the girl who nursed me gently for a day.

The window rattles in its pane. In the soft linens of my bed, I feel sleepy but I must stay awake: influenza is at our door, on the steps of all the houses near Embley, and my heart skips because I've been permitted to help. I am needed.

I am sixteen years old, nursing our ill servants, enjoying the pace and rhythm of it. Memories resurface of Mother smoothing a blanket down my legs, a hand on my forehead.

In total ten of our servants are sick, plus my mother and two cousins, and they all become my patients. Cook helps me as best she can. Broth, tea, bread, jellies. Together we drag in the linens from outside and poke the dirty clothes into the boiler. She does all this cheerfully – I think she likes having the place practically to herself. Neither she nor I become ill and for the first time I feel useful – God is speaking directly to me. But that's not quite right. It's as though He is *seeing* through me and urging me to use my gifts for good. It's a feeling like feathers at the edges of my mind, fragile, likely to slip away.

And through Him I observe the sweat, the moans, the terrible red and purple of my patients' faces. Bodies appear to vibrate then become still under the bedclothes, and the coughs are sharp and loud in the passageways. This is all a part of His plan for me. Not the endless society months in London, the vases and hat trimming, the embroidery hoops like little shields.

In bed at night my exhausted self buzzes. I sleep with the windows open and heavy bedclothes upon me. My new room is unadorned, in a part of the house I rarely visit, but in it my body feels compact and fit for purpose. I am no bigger or richer than I ought to be, here in this room, and freedom beckons – no fuss, no interruptions, no invitations. I can let my mind have its conversation with God, a deep exchange that wends through me like a breeze through grass. In the Gospel of Luke, there's a parable about a woman who has ten coins but loses one. She lights a lamp and overturns the furniture and sweeps her house till she finds the drachma. *Actions*, I whisper in the dark. Only then can the woman in the parable celebrate. Accomplishments – not crocheting nosegays onto cushions. It isn't enough to ride in a carriage with Mother and Parthe and deliver soup to the poor people in our village, to give out money. It isn't even enough to nurse our servants through this influenza, as it will soon be over and I'll no longer be of use. Actions. Resolutions. Light the lamp and pick up the broom.

After the flu has passed, Mother and Father order all the beds to be stripped and the linens burnt, far away from the house. Mother flings open the windows and sits at the pianoforte for an hour as though she can blast the sickness out, sound and sight.

In Wellow, where people have died, the funerals take place over several weeks, and I climb the big cedar tree to watch the chimneys smoke. A severe winter chill has descended on the village. Amid the grief of the funerals, a thought is born: curing others cures me. I keep this to myself.

Parthe dreams such loud and frightening dreams. She jolts me in the morning until I open my eyes to listen: how she waded through swamps in her dresses, trying to find me, while she fought off spiders and eels. Bill, who brings the coal, says that if you dream too long without animals, death is surely close. I'm glad to know that Parthe is safe.

When I think about Mother and Father tucked away in their rooms, not knowing for sure that they pray at night as I do, I try to picture their dreams run through with baboons and frogs and fish and mice.

It takes a long time for the linens to burn. In the village, the chimneys are fast at work, our sheets and pillow slips being incinerated before my tired eyes.

Silas

I catch sight of a basket on the tiled floor in the passageway and in it a mound of ladies' clothes, white and lemon-yellow, a marching pattern of flowers. Mabel strides over it, says she is fetching some herbs from the garden. I am alone again. I get up and feel the pleasure of the soft fabrics through my fingers.

The start of spring is upon me. Ten years old, I clamber across the field that lies to the east of our house. Seeds from the golden grass shake loose and catch in my socks, depositing themselves there like precious metals. If I make it home in time, I'll see my mother before she wanders, unsteadily, off to bed. I spent the afternoon with my friend Paul and have been out too long – I know that. I get it into my head that my mother will never be angry with me because of her condition, and I feel ashamed for thinking it. The condition makes her mellow, usually.

My childhood home. I burst through the front door. I have to kick at the bottom of it, near the frame, and, as I do, some of the grass seeds scatter and end up in the fibres of the rug.

It's all right, I think, *I can find them later.*

'I'm home,' I say. 'Ma!'

It's too loud, I'm too loud, my boots are coarse like my voice. Coming home in this way was a mistake. 'Mummy?'

Somehow that works, the quieter call. She pops her head around the wall that separates the hallway from the front room. 'You're here,' she says. She wears the faded pink bonnet that she hasn't let us wash in weeks. *Does it hurt if we take it from you?*

As quickly as I can, I start to unlace my boots to sit upright beside the door. I urge my fingers to work faster. 'Hello,' I say. 'Yes, I'm here.'

Sometimes Mother doesn't get out of bed for days. Tucked away, as though she's hibernating from Sunday onwards, right after we get home from church, till Tuesday or Wednesday. Sometimes she is lively all morning and in the afternoon makes me a cup of tea. Then she withers like fruit by the weekend and I do not see her, my father saying, *No, you mustn't go in there*, in his gentle, wheaty voice.

The next day: a sunny morning in Beaconsfield. The mist rises off the hillside, off the valley. Our village is in a halo and I long to be let out of the house. My mother is not up. I watch Pa drive a knife into a loaf of bread. He cuts off two slices, gives me the larger of the two, then folds the second one into paper. He has it in him too, that urge to be outside. I can never sit still at the table, or during church. He doesn't try to change this about me.

He's made the bread himself, from memory – Ma must have taught him. When I say she hasn't yet risen from bed that day, I mean that she's unlikely to rise all day. If we were to notice her in the doorway in her nightdress and stockings, well, both of us would be forced to hide our surprise, clear the papers from her chair, set a plate at the table and pretend that she had made the loaf.

I will take my slice of bread with me when I go to meet Paul on the high road – I never have other boys around the house. Paul – orphaned, tall, tucked-in and combed-back – lives with his aunt and uncle on the other side of the village. He is ten, or maybe he is eleven too. He is well fed but I figure I won't eat the bread till I see him and offer him a corner.

'Goodbye, Ma,' I whisper. The horror if I were to wake her.

My father hops up and around the table to stir at a pot on the stove. The muscles of his broad back, under his brown shirt, are moving with the motion of the spoon. Mothers do this sort of work, not fathers. Pa is bearded, enormous, somehow delicate. Most days he is at the brickworks.

'Stay right,' he says. 'Be good.'

I tell him I will.

Paul stands with his knees apart. He stares at the ground between his feet. I want us to be out all day. We'll go to the stream and poke around at the leather suitcase we found wedged in the rocks there yesterday. We'd resisted our desire to open the latches straight away, because to take up all the joy in that moment would be to discard it. Maybe we will make our way to the Parley farm and eat all the apples. Once, Paul vomited in a ditch not far from where the apples dropped from the trees the Parleys tend. After he'd done it, we fell about laughing, and for a time Paul swore off apples, but that didn't last long.

The suitcase: it's the sort of thing we know not to talk about in front of other children, or our families, not even each other in case we break the spell. Having been called silly, impulsive, thick in the head by my Sunday School teacher, I think of my capacity to delay opening the suitcase – because I know it will be better doled out, slowly and evenly – and it makes me proud.

'You all right?' Paul asks when he sees me, a grin on his face.

'Yeah, you?'

He nods.

'Shall we?'

And that is that. Off we go into the cool morning. I see a hare tick-tock on its paws on the roadside. The bread is a promise in my pocket, and my thoughts spin out to my mother in the cottage. She won't have risen by now, so I should stop thinking that she might have. I follow Paul, and sometimes he follows me, through the thicket of woods and along the top of a golden ridge above our village – a meadow of long, wavy grass. I take in the market square and the church with its blue-painted sign. The stream is past the town and when we get there the slow-rising sun is hidden by the trees. We push our way through hedges and over rocks half in and half out of the ground.

'I see it. It's still there.'

'So do I,' Paul says. 'I was worried for a bit. Were you?'

I was. 'Me too,' I tell him, because I'm softening for being truthful. It's appealing to me more and more.

We dragged the suitcase out of the river yesterday, not knowing how long it had been there or where it had come from. Set it on the curve of the dry bank to sit all day and night till we came back. We thought if it was not here today then the traveller or salesman or whoever it might belong to had collected it – and wouldn't that have been a disappointment, but also a great mystery in itself. And we'd have been absolved from stealing it. Sunlight wriggles on the leaves at the top of the stream. Paul and I are squatting on a pair of rocks, side by side, and we stare at the suitcase. I dip my fingers in the river and feel them bitten with the cold water.

'Who goes first?' Paul asks.

'You can.'

He doesn't question this, hopping down from his spot to

work on the latches. The left one opens easily with a click, then he stands aside for me. *Click* goes the latch on the right, wet and icy beneath my thumb and forefinger. Did a rich man own this? It's a very nice suitcase.

We each take a corner of the lid. I glance around, imagining footsteps, or the hush-hush of a fox across the grass.

'Wait,' I say. 'I brought bread.'

'After,' Paul says. His eyes do not leave the case.

And inside it is all: *soft*. My first instinct is to plunge my hand right in. Pinks and lemons, a white like cow's milk, and pale grey cloth. A nightgown that slithers between Paul's fingers. A green skirt. A thin bonnet, stockings, undershirts, a shawl with pockets.

Paul shrieks and balls up the nightgown, throws it into my chest.

I toss it back.

We unpack the contents, some of it wet, and lay everything out on the grass. We weigh down the corners with stones and flatten the ghosts of the bodies. I'm waiting for the sun to hit the clothes, as though that will solve the mystery.

'Who's it for?' Paul asks.

'It's all big,' I say.

'Like for a mother, I think.'

'I'm not sure.'

Paul shakes his head. 'They must belong to someone. Up there or down there.'

'Have you ever noticed anybody in town wearing this?' I ask, holding up the shawl. 'Think, Paul.'

Think, Silas.

We could take them to the constable. That would make sense. But then he'd want to know why we had touched the things first – it would be obvious we had. I picture my mother's face if I were to arrive home with the constable at my elbow.

'Oh,' she would say. *Oh.* Flustered and inviting him in then searching for the tea things. Lid on, lid off, lid on, lid off. She could do that pattern for minutes at a time without knowing it, while she tried to get it right, whatever that meant to her, whatever message was playing out in her mind. And she might be furious even if I tried to explain I'd done nothing wrong, not really.

I blurt out, 'I want to take these home to Ma.'

Paul's eyes are wide on me. 'What if the person who owns them sees them on her?'

'She doesn't leave the house, does she,' I say, 'so that won't happen.'

Paul hops his way across the stream. 'What about my mother?' he calls out.

I must be careful. I try to think what Pa would say. 'I didn't think you saw her anymore.'

'I see her,' Paul says. He brings himself up tall, up on a rock like a statue. 'But you're right – you keep them. My mother doesn't need these silly things.'

Florence

I swore off marriage when I was thirty years old. Before that, I might have been persuaded by a man who could match me for faith and for adventure. God needed people like me with good intentions and a desire to take risks. A fraction more of a push from a man towards marriage, something more to offer, and perhaps I would have said yes. Tantalising, tempting, to surrender and say yes. A moment of liberation that an almost-falling man must feel before he lets go of the sharp edge of a bridge.

Signs that went unnoticed by others showed themselves to me. Parthe used to watch me swim in the Derwent. I sensed the rocks fall away from under me and I urged myself on, legs pushing at the glacial water. I sensed terrible eels at my ankles (nothing frightened my sister and me more than the manic eyes and slimy whip of an eel's body). Parthe didn't dare scream, which would have risked people at the house knowing that we were, indeed, in the river. I fought against the slow current and panicked and, very briefly, slipped under the mud-fearsome water. I felt the right direction to take and I trusted the rocks, that another would be laid beneath my feet at the moment I needed it. When I drew myself up onto the bank, the sun was already working to warm my shoulders and face.

'You nearly drowned,' she said.

'It wasn't that close, nothing like that.' I found my boots and dress. I tried to catch my breath.

I was proud of her comment, though – *drowned* – that she thought me so close to death but I had saved myself. It was faith I had, in deeper stores than Parthe, that I wouldn't die in the mucky river before teatime. It was like this: chance, opportunity. The men in the War Office preparing for the Crimean War sought me out. In time they came to give me a role that no woman had ever held. I saw the words in a letter: *Superintendent of the Female Nursing Establishment*. Unofficially, I would be equivalent to a major. Later still, unofficially, a full colonel.

I felt my way onto the packet steamer and, as we separated ourselves from the earth and went forth across the sea, I prayed like I had as a child: *Give me this day my work to do. Give me this day to do Thy work.* I crossed the English Channel, going to Marseilles and then to Scutari with my flock of newborn nurses. And the waves were like stones beneath our feet.

At the Barrack Hospital in Scutari, they said I was odd. I liked to watch the surgeons. Me in the corner with my arms folded, not getting in the way – so why shouldn't I stand silently and witness a man having his insides rearranged? What, precisely, was the problem with beholding a poor soldier on a stretcher going through an amputation? (Eventually I bought screens, which nobody before me had thought to do, so the soldier could have some privacy, and also not frighten the next wretched patient to death.) I believed those men deserved a witness, and I deserved an opportunity to know how to help the next one. Observing was an action. Deeds, not words. Covered in blood and nearly asphyxiated by the stench of the hospital, I recalled an old aunt who'd tried to convince me that anything, even a dinner party, could be done to the glory of God. But here I solved problems. I argued for more – more money, more blankets, more soap, a shipment of chamberpots to replace the last lot that slid into the Black Sea. (Such incompetence. Who might I have tipped into the sea?)

I pooled my money with donations from the readers of a newspaper owned by Mr Macdonald, and together he and I went to the bazaars of Constantinople to search for what was needed and haggle with the Turks at the stalls, which were piled high with figs, apricots, quinces, lemons and grapes. We found blankets, pots, bowls, knives, spoons, and paper and ink for the nurses. Give them something to do and who knows what sort of news they might disseminate homewards. And, yes, lamps. We bought lamps too.

Mr Macdonald became rather worldly when we were out on one of our adventures and I noted his strong features and decisive manner while he gestured to a shopkeeper, an orange in one hand. I thought of my mother and what she would say if she saw me on the arm of a man who was not my husband or my kin, with exotic people in their fine dresses and cloaks swirling all around us, pushing into me. I was never afraid.

A patient's room must be aired. The air inside must be fresh, ventilated, clean and not befouled. Sleep with the windows open, even in winter. A draught is different and must be managed separately – do not let the fear of a draught stop you from opening the windows. Do not ask a patient to turn their head towards you. Do not speak in such a way that a patient feels he must strain to catch your words. Do not speak about a patient while he is in earshot. Do not ask him to remember anything about his treatment – this will cause him discomfort. Alleviate patients' distress by keeping them warm, by asking no questions. Let them rest. Let the light in. Ventilate the room. Clean the utensils. Change the sheets yourself and do it quickly, without comment. Open the windows. Stop the chimney from smoking by working the fire at its base. Let the air in. The part I was trying hardest to impress upon my young nurses was how much the small details matter. In a ventilated room a man will have peace in his mind to think of his family, his wife if he has one, their home together. Life will be, however briefly, pleasant.

I sweep beside Mr Ryan's bed. He is twenty-nine years old, a former schoolteacher from Leeds. 'Mr Ryan,' I say, 'I'm going to turn you gently now.'

He makes no sound, has made no sound the whole time I've been caring for him at Scutari. A shell went off behind his shoulder; his hearing is mostly gone and, most likely, his mind. He carries the half-look I have come to recognise. I make it my duty, which it is indeed, to stare right into Mr Ryan's eyes so I can remember him.

Silas

My body is a disaster. The sight of my reflection in Miss Nightingale's front hall gave me a fright: I haven't been whole for such a long time. When I met Jean and was a soldier in the army, wearing my red uniform – then I looked smart and in one piece. Before the mud; before that freezing war-winter; before I didn't wash my face for weeks, or shave, or clean my shirt. They gave us raw meat, rice, sugar and rum. Some salted pork, though not much. They gave us coffee but it was up to us to roast it, figure out ways to grind it up. Before all that: I wore my hat and belt, and I wished my father could have seen me the day before I set foot in the river that led to the Black Sea.

Me, well, I was too terrified to get in. It was running

red past me, the water lapping at the toes of my boots. I threw myself to the ground and the mud was wet against my cheek. You'd think the mud would be the least of a man's problems but honestly it was murder – so cold and thick it threatened to eat me alive. The sounds of heavy fire sailed over my head, where chaos was knocking around. Fear clattered through my skull.

A man on a horse galloped behind me and yelled. In the depths of his voice I could hear a call for somebody back home – because the bodies were piling up. He could see that as well as I. My ammunition – comfort in that word *my*, but also obligation and fury at it too – was a weight pressing into my back.

In the distance, a curl of smoke rose above a village. In lines two deep, more British troops emerged from the smoke and around them ran a pair of hounds chasing hares through the muck. And I was thinking of being a child back home with Paul when we stalked pale grey bodies through the woods in the laneways. Silent deaths – those bony bunnies – in the mouths of the village dogs while we ran beside them in the lane.

I turned my head to the side, moving the mud from the outside of one cheek to another, and I saw tall figures in uniform. I watched as some of them dropped silently and gracefully, like dancers, the bullets arriving like a touch to the shoulder. I wondered if that touch would come for me. (Jean's hand taking hold of mine and urging it down the length of her body, to where she wanted it.) Nowhere for me to fall to earth. Already here.

But when has anybody been able to stay in the mud forever? A man has to cross that river. I saw other soldiers rise from the banks. Together, our eyes took in the swift current, flicking left to right, left to right. We had our ammunition pouches, so precious to us, and where else to put mine but above my head, my rifle too. I fitted mine into that snug place at the top of my spine across my shoulders and I stepped into the river. It was a stream, I told myself. Around me: curses and wails. But the river: just another stream. Violent water. Icy shock. But a stream in Beaconsfield and is Paul anywhere to be found? My father? A man could get his head blown off for thinking of his pa and his blessed childhood with its dainty bodies of water while bullets zigged through the air. A rough current surged around my shins, then my thighs, then my waist. Oh, truly the coldest water of my life on the barest, softest parts of me. Nothing prepared me for the way it seized me, wrapped around my middle, the way it came for me. I was close to laughter – the thought that, after all this, freezing water might be my undoing.

So I breathed, nothing special, but I reminded myself of it. I was now wet up to my chest, sliding and going under briefly, a bolt of shock like kicking out a leg in bed, half awake. I held on to that rifle and that pouch, not knowing what would be left of it when I got to the other side. The dogs' barking, the soldier on the horse now behind me, and I was seeing men slip the same as I'd been doing but not getting up again. Drowning sometimes mere seconds after walking off the land. Not for me to try to help them. I had no energy left to be useful and heroic, though I wanted to be. One fellow's wet black head made its own hole in the water beside me and then he was through it, and gone.

My body twitched and simmered. I was a blur, nothing solid, as common as a reed. I slipped under again, by accident, saw nothing and struck back up to the surface with a mouthful of the murderous water. My rifle was in my arms now, the pouch too, staring at me as if we were family, as if we owed each other something. The smoke and the fires blazed up ahead, against the late-afternoon sky. In seconds I would be on the other side. I could be safe. I felt a leg kick into mine and fingers at my elbow. That hand wanted me, I was sure of it. I surged forward. No body other than mine could exist right now. And in a flash I thought I saw Paul perched on a rock in the sun. His bare feet were flattened against the stone. He pointed his toes towards the water but kept them from being lapped by the tender waves. Our precious suitcase wasn't yet opened. It wasn't yet found. It still belonged to its owner, who was warm and dry in her dresses. A message in that for me, I thought, a lesson about being whole. I was about to grasp the lesson – it was moving towards me on the current. I was so close to the bank and I felt the water getting lower and lower around my body.

And then a hot flare went off in my left side and I thought, *Oh, a nasty stick caught in an undertow has come to pierce me.* But indeed I'd been shot and the lesson drifted away. I felt somebody's grip under my arms.

'I'm shot,' I said.

That somebody fought the current for me and I saw how the bank edged closer while the whole river rushed into my chest.

For a time I'm aware of Mabel doing chores in the drawing room. The house is mostly still. I hear a pipe in distress and the wind in the almost-dark outside. My head rests on a cushion. Although I have no sense of Miss Nightingale's movements upstairs, I feel her presence. She is awake as I am, here in this pretty house. Tired again, so tired. I could fall asleep now, forever, but then what? The forever wouldn't last. It would simply be another of my hibernations and I would wake up, not alone this time, but still without answers.

I toss the blanket from my knees. In seconds I'm upstairs but in truth it's probably taken longer. Sneaking is what I'm doing now, so Mabel doesn't catch me. She wants me to rest, nothing more. On the landing, I pass a vase of white flowers in water; I keep a fist clamped to my side as the river surges over me, towards me, into me, time and again. A torment to be killed but to never fully die.

Down the hall I locate Miss Nightingale's room, still hearing nothing from inside. I drop to my knees and lay my ear against her bedroom door. A word – *mother* – rushes into me like clean water.

'Miss Nightingale? Please listen. What did Jean do to me?'

II

The English Channel
October 1854

Jean

For the first time Jean was seeing Miss Nightingale up close – practical-looking, plain, dignified. Her eyes were never at rest. Just like Jean she was in a bonnet, dress and cloak. Spotless, immaculate on the ship to Scutari. Years later, Jean could never recall in detail the background, what had been going on around them when she first met Miss N. Like those paintings that her old boss Mr Turner had hung in the drawing room where some parts were in focus and other parts were blurred. It took energy to shift your eyes away from what was so vital at its centre.

A fine mist, spray from the ocean, was on Miss N's face and shawl while she talked to Jean and the other women who had come to join her. The nurses stood with shoulders squared and noses tipped upwards, defiance in every gesture. They had all beaten something to be here and perhaps they observed one another, wondering about the particulars, the lives the other girls must have led, lives that from this day on might end up foreshortened. Jean wanted to know whose story she would learn, which girl might end up a friend – could she do that? Because part of her also turned away, inside, from what would have once been a joy – meeting other young women and learning their names. Because what if she met some sadness in them that matched or exceeded her own?

Jean fixed her eyes on Miss N, whose body seemed fashioned so straight and tall: not a bone out of place, or even a thought. Jean felt herself wishing for the resolve Miss N appeared to have.

Miss N was thirty-four years old. Jean was twenty-four. To escape properly she had to keep her feet on this deck. So small, so afraid and so absolutely sure that she'd made an awful mistake.

They rolled on.

The wind thrust itself at the night boat. A girl to the left of Miss N caught Jean's eye.

'I'm Cora.'

'Jean Frawley.'

Best to pretend she'd known adventure before. In her mind, Jean spun a story to recount in case Cora asked her.

In truth, Jean had never been on a ship, never been anywhere. She took one last glimpse at the watery distance that was expanding between herself and home.

Later, another boat: down the Rhône River to Avignon. Jean had imagined the beds on board would be luxurious, with gleaming dinner plates piled high with meat and bowls with pudding, the lights of foreign cities passing by in the night. Instead the vessel was filled with cockroaches that fled from corner to corner, over tables and onto the underside of ladders and door handles. At supper on the first night, a cockroach scuttled over the arm of Louise, a mouse of a nurse from Plymouth with a bald patch in her hair, and Jean saw Louise go still then fling her arm out to the side. The insect went flying before she resumed her dinner.

One of the nurses – Georgina, squinting face, glossy blonde hair – was unwell and refused to come out of her room. It was up to Jean and Louise to bring her tea, even while the boat rocked and glugged Jean's insides about. If she thought very hard about her stomach, which she was trying to keep as empty as a bowl, she got the roiling feeling too.

'Come on, Georgina,' Jean said at her door. 'Please let us in.'

A groan.

'Should we tell Miss Nightingale?' Louise asked.

Jean had wondered too but knew it would sound like the problems of little girls clamouring desperately to find an adult in charge. After all, they would face worse than this.

Jean rapped her knuckles on the door. 'You need some tea.'

Georgina's deep voice: 'Not now. I can't get up.'

'Be a good girl. Come on, don't be silly. You'll feel better and stronger if you have something.' Words that might have coaxed Benjamin or Anna when Jean had nursed Mr Turner's children.

Then the sound of something being thrown at the door.

'Oh, all right,' Jean said, but what she was thinking was, *No need to be so stupid, so dramatic, we're all feeling it, she's worse than a child, and perhaps I should indeed tell Miss N that one of her nurses is already hopeless.*

'Come on, Louise.' Jean turned the door knob and pushed hard, knowing Louise was not at her side but back against the wall of the corridor, her shoulders turning in on themselves.

'Leave her be,' Louise was saying, holding the cup of tea.

But Jean was already inside.

'Don't,' Georgina said feebly, as though reading Jean's mind about the state of things.

'Well, I'm here now, I'm afraid.' Jean was moving quickly. The corner of the room thrummed with the smell of vomit. A brown dress had been bunched up and discarded on the bed; Georgina was on her side in her undergarments with her Derry wrapper loosely tied across her front. Jean saw that she'd tried to cover the bucket of sick with a straw bonnet.

'Louise, look,' Jean said over her shoulder, as Louise remained in the corridor. 'The bucket is wearing a hat!'

Jean was trying her best. *Good God, the stench*, she thought, *Georgina, you poor girl*. Jean came round to the bed, up as close as she could manage. Georgina's skin was wet at the temples and forehead, wet around the mouth. Jean told her she should sit up and get fresh air, right now, and that they would help her. Fresh air being the only thing for it. The day was not yet over and Georgina could catch some light across the river. Imagine the good it would do. But in truth Jean knew that up on the decks it was hardly safe and nothing short of freezing, the air not in the slightest bit still or sweet. She turned and went round behind Georgina and lifted her under the armpits.

'There you go,' Jean said, achieving nothing.

Georgina slumped to one side against her pillow. The thing about ill children, Jean thought, was how much they wanted to forget their illness. Benjamin had loved a joke and Anna loved her box of buttons and beads at the table whenever Jean took her temperature.

'You're not the only one, Georgina.' Jean meant it kindly. Several women hadn't left their rooms all day, too ill to come up to the deck. Miss Nightingale herself hadn't been seen. The passage through the waters now seemingly endless. Great strong solid Cora hadn't had so much as a hiccup, and Jean thanked her own strong constitution too, and her capacity to go long stretches without eating.

Later still, on the train that arrowed through fields from Avignon to Marseilles, where they would spend a couple of nights, those days on the boat – which had seemed so unpleasant, so long and troubling – faded. The sun was high in the sky, teapot-blue with oily-looking clouds, when the train pulled into Marseilles and Jean walked off. Georgina was somewhere up ahead. After a few moments on solid ground Jean felt sure-footed again. Many of them were poor girls like her, although she'd learnt quickly that Cora and Mary and a few others came from money. Georgina too had enjoyed a rather cosseted life before she found Miss N's advertisement in a newspaper and somehow persuaded her family to let her go. The waves washed all that away, making that life no longer possible.

Her feet on the earth, her bags at her side, Jean caught sight of Miss N on the railway platform, radiating health and light.

On the morning in Marseilles that Jean, Mary and Georgina were meant to meet the soldier, Miss N was in fine spirits. Jean didn't ask the name of the soldier – Miss N knew all sorts of men in the War Office and one of them had arranged it all. It was enough to be invited out into Marseilles to talk to somebody new. Jean had to push the next ship out of her mind. She thought she would be eager to keep moving to Scutari but something about being back on land had stalled things for her and given her a low-humming fright.

They walked two by two along the pavement, dipping onto the road whenever Miss N did to avoid a child, a dog, a cart. The girls kept up with her like ducklings.

Miss N was beside Jean.

'Did you sleep well?' Jean asked because she herself had slept terribly.

'Fine, thank you. And you?'

'Very well, thank you, Miss Nightingale.'

It had been too hot, too cold. She tossed and turned while fears and grief came upon her like a growing forest, foliage blooming and unfurling in her mind's eye. At one point she felt a dent in the bedclothes on her thigh. It was a light, round pressure like a cat settling in for the night, and Jean held her breath and didn't open her eyes. A girl called Catherine had mentioned a ghost at dinner the night before. *The man downstairs said not to worry about the ghost. He told me it's just a boy and perfectly harmless.* Jean had stared. Idiotic Catherine. No ghost. But no cat either.

Miss N gestured to indicate they ought to pause for a trio of carriages to pass. Jean, Mary and Georgina waited for her signal and then crossed the road.

Miss N said, 'It wouldn't do to be squashed before we've left the continent, would it?'

They giggled.

She could tell a little joke, then. Always a surprise.

Not for the first time, Jean considered the pull of this woman and her energy – small, fierce, devout, as bright as sunlight. Miss N had bought herself a pair of binoculars made of blackened brass and she wore them now on a string around her neck, every few moments lifting them to her face to peer at the locals. Surely these people could see she was a strange and powerful creature. Jean wanted to feel the heft of those binoculars for herself, fit them to her eyes. Jean's own world before her time here (this place, this adventure, this foreign land) had not been vast. Her parents were neither curious nor cruel but they had no money and she'd often wondered at the fact of her being their only child – the streams of invisible pain that might have run beneath their feet. Growing up, Jean knew that the hem of the world was close by.

As they passed stalls and gardens, Miss N described the houses she'd lived in as a child – vast lawns, countless servants, endless parties, trips to Egypt and Germany and Greece. Miss N said matter-of-factly that she had learnt Hebrew so she could read the Bible in the language and come to know God that way. She motioned to the morning sky and talked about books written by a scientist named Mary Somerville that had taught her about the path of the moon – one called *Mechanism of the Heavens* and one called *On the Connexion of the Physical Sciences*. These words conjured no images for Jean. But awe, yes, and envy in spades. To get the job, Jean hadn't been required to show proof of her schooling or her faith – imagine having to lay out for Miss N the last time God had revealed Himself to her! Which was never.

Rose and Mrs McLean and all the girls at the boarding house wouldn't have found time their whole lives to agonise over having dozens of servants and what it all *meant*.

As a nurse, Jean was to obey Miss N in everything, including caring for each soldier no matter his religion. No proselytising. A chaplain could be summoned for that sort of comfort. A curious thing, Jean thought, for a woman who so loved God to want her nurses to stay quiet on the matter. But relief too: she wouldn't be asked to relieve a soldier of his burdens.

She glanced at the other women and resolved to try to unburden herself to at least one of them: to perhaps tell a new friend that Benjamin Turner, just four years old, had died of scarlet fever while he was in Jean's care. Things were alive and then they were not. Jean was about to face this again in Turkey, this and more. Who would remember her? Plenty of people would talk about Benjamin for years, would recall the beautiful boy. His parents; his sister, Anna. Jean felt the little story of his body running through her now. She imagined how the servants spent their hours at the house where she had worked as Anna and Benjamin's governess for ten months – how they might tidy Benjamin's side of the nursery, then wait for instructions from Mr Turner about which objects to discard and which to keep forever. The loss of a child. A museum in the making. Perhaps even Cook would keep her morning encounters with Benjamin close by while she tried to inch the Turners forward into their new life. Cook had once told Jean that the boy's cheeks reminded her of two half-circles of creamy cheese. Words kept people alive, Jean thought. A rod of sadness went through her chest.

Miss N kept up a good pace. She wasn't breathless with all that chatter: this spa town and that spa town; a whole winter in Rome, where Miss N stood beneath the Sistine Chapel and also saw the Pope climb into his carriage. An adventure to the Luxor Temple, which she didn't much like, actually. Months and months of it all, it seemed.

While they walked she never asked the girls about their families, which was not her job, but surely she could tell how much they enjoyed her stories. Cora, who had five brothers, had already learnt that Miss Nightingale's parents had longed for a son and more than once she'd told them to pretend she was one. Jean thought about Mr Turner and his work as a lawyer. His first wife had died and he'd remarried. His new wife, the one Jean had known, was Mrs Orla Turner, who drifted in and out of rooms with a book in hand. She had a cheerful demeanour, yes, but no particular chores to do, meetings to attend, problems to solve. And the children were taken care of.

Again: Benjamin.

Thoughts of him were a horse running towards her, unstoppable and fierce. In her dreams he was alive and cheerful on the garden seat. He was at the table, passing her a spoon. He was running ahead along the Serpentine, the twisting green of the grass flashing beneath his boots with each footfall.

A blow when Jean had woken that morning on her narrow bed in the Marseilles hotel to recall that he had died. The truth came thudding in and she felt she might crumble. If she was not cut out for the work at Scutari she needed to know as much now and not in two days' time. A stop in Marseilles simply made the next part harder to picture.

Jean turned her face to the sky and nodded at a man who tipped his hat to their party of four. Jean knew this feeling: she was losing her nerve. She needed momentum, no time to stop and think. Every block or so, Miss N took from her pocket a notebook and a pencil and jotted things down. At one point, because of the silence, Jean focused on two sisters playing in the front garden of a majestic house. A woman – maybe the governess – walked in loops behind them. The children trotted up to drop objects into her palms, then ran away to gather more, as if for safekeeping. Jean found comfort in that simple action.

She glanced at the fast-walking Miss N and caught the side of her face, which was directed forward, Jean finally detecting a heart rate hitched higher from the exertion. Nagging at Jean now, part of this problem with her failing nerve, was the first little lie that got her into the Turners' house, which led to another, and then another. And then the advertisement for nurses that she found in the newspaper, and an interview in London, which had taken place in an unknown, grand house that overlooked Regent's Park, where a stern lady fired questions at Jean and six other girls. Jean felt like the last woman standing. She was good at thinking on her feet, good at listing examples of why ventilation, cleanliness, good diet and distance between patients were next to godliness. She turned her charm on the bossy woman, figuring that Miss N probably needed to fill the spots for Scutari fast. Jean had expected hundreds of girls. But, no, the final party could have fitted inside any schoolroom around the country. Not quite a neat forty. A Biblical number, it seemed, and maybe Miss N had wanted it that way.

And now here she was in Marseilles trotting beside Miss N, who was clever, magnetic, commanding.

To her, Jean said, 'This will be interesting. To meet a soldier who has come from the Crimea.'

'Yes, indeed. A great opportunity to hear from a soldier who is doing the reverse of our journey, back to England.'

Mary asked, 'What happened to him?'

'Deployed back home for now.'

'Oh,' Jean said. *Home.*

'Keep up, please,' Miss N told them. 'Not far to go.'

And Jean heard her own voice in there, somewhere in the past, urging Anna and Benjamin to make it home from the park before the sun went down.

———

The café where they would meet the soldier stood on a corner block behind a black iron fence. It was a two-storey building, stone walls painted dark orange, with pastel-brick steps and archways. A pretty spot, another in a long line of unfamiliar and entrancing places that were revealing themselves to Jean. Above them was a cold sky and huge bare trees that hugged the pathway to the entrance.

'Isn't this nice?' Mary said, and Georgina agreed that it was.

Jean was excited for coffee in a warm hotel, excited to be chosen although she had experienced rushes of horror at what the soldier might reveal to them all. She would keep her face set – she shuffled to hide a bit behind Mary – and practise an expression that was pure for listening, betraying nothing.

Mary reached over and tucked a strand of Jean's hair behind her ear. 'You, my girl – people at home must tell you you're pretty.'

Jean smiled. 'Not once,' she said. She gathered her skirt and walked up and into a black-and-white-tiled foyer.

Miss N approached a man stationed inside the glass doors to the restaurant. In the presence of staff, in this gleaming place, Jean glimpsed Miss N's breeding, her comfort, her ease at speaking French. In the café were more than a dozen small tables topped with grey marble, black chairs, and plants in tall pots. People leant forward to sip at cups like graceful birds at a water hole. Jean was at sea all over again (what to do with her hands, how to order and how would they pay?) but she vowed to mirror what the others did while Miss N said something low in French that made the waiter seem to stand up straighter, pausing with his pen and notebook for her to speak again.

Nightingale was the word Jean heard when the whole room stilled around her, clear and bright, when she first saw the soldier across the café. He rose from his seat and caught not Miss N's eyes, but hers. In his jacket and fawn-coloured trousers, he wasn't tall but he was solid with dark hair and shining eyes. He had an open face that was somehow sad, with a not-quite smile. But he nodded at her as if he knew.

Desire.

She breathed out.

It was hunger she felt, hunger she remembered.

The waiter motioned for their group to move to the table. The other guests were dressed in their jewels, their bird colours and feathers. The nod from the man and the colours brought the room back to life again in a dizzying swirl. Glances – just briefly, from a few diners – at their party, dressed in brown dresses, grey shawls and mantles, headed by Miss N.

The café was a ship. All those tables and tucked-in chairs and waiters to navigate while her face burnt. Jean was unsteady across its surface, propelling herself towards the man, whose eyes were on her. A shimmering in her chest, a flutter at her throat. Her fingertips tingled and she was sure he could tell. Scents in the high-ceilinged room – coffee, bread, lemon, perfume.

'Sergeant Silas Bradley,' Miss N said.

He took his eyes from Jean. 'Ma'am, Miss Nightingale, a pleasure to meet you.'

She shook his hand. 'Miss Mary Boyd and Miss Georgina Wickham – both, Mr Bradley, are about to journey to nurse your fellow soldiers.'

'Pleased to meet you,' Mary said. She and Georgina arranged themselves behind two of the chairs.

Jean had stopped a few paces behind the others. Miss N had to swivel to find her, showing a flash of annoyance at this minuscule obstacle. 'And this is Miss Jean Frawley.'

'Ma'am.'

'Mr Bradley.'

'Miss Frawley is another of the fine nurses accompanying me to Scutari.'

Struck, still, by the handsomeness of the man's face and working hard to keep from blushing, a tiny part of Jean was able to feel emboldened. That word *fine* coming from Miss N gave Jean pause – that possibly Miss N was playing a bit here, too, and was more nervous than one might think. Maybe saying out loud that somebody was a good nurse was a way of hoping they were.

'The Crimea. Well.' His attention on Miss N. 'Let me tell you what it's like.'

They took their seats at the round table: Georgina sat to Jean's left, then Mr Bradley to Georgina's left, talking softly to Miss N and Mary beside him. Each time Jean glanced up, there he was. His brown eyes on her as though he was *waiting*. When he and Miss N spoke, it was effortless. Compared with the words Jean could manage during those first moments, Mr Bradley and Miss N would have seemed like friends – perhaps Miss N was a few years older than he was? Through her whirling thoughts, Jean heard him listing their rations. The waiter delivered their coffee and Jean watched Mr Bradley stir the pearl-handled spoon through it, catching sight of a brass ring on his smallest finger. He made a joke about coffee rations. Jean heard herself laughing. He described the snow in Sebastopol, said he'd spare them the details of what cholera did to a man.

Miss N motioned around the restaurant. 'On account of the other diners today? Or because of my young nurses? Because they will find out soon enough.'

He shook his head. 'The other patrons.' He turned first to Georgina, then to Mary, asking about their nursing experience and where they had come from. Jean's face warmed; she could feel the redness there. She prayed he would know her mind and ask her nothing.

And he did.

Mary and Georgina excused themselves and swished their way to the bathrooms, quite enjoying themselves and very much at home in a place such as this. By the time the coffee was finished, Miss N and Mr Bradley were speaking almost solely to each other. Jean didn't mind. She listened to them talk freely about supplies that had been lost at sea, about medical officers outpaced by disease. All the while Jean's left hand felt magnetised by the soldier's right hand across the table. He had a way of moving it gently from a fist to an open palm and back again while he spoke, and it seemed to beckon her. When he gazed at her she felt swallowed whole. And Miss N prattled on, appearing not to notice.

Later, outside in the freezing air, he stood next to Jean at the top of the stairs. She couldn't command her fingers to button her coat. He was at her elbow and she feared he would try to help. If he did, surely the others who were halfway down the steps would see her expression. But he watched and waited till she pushed the final button through.

'I didn't get a chance to ask about your experiences as a nurse and what's brought you here.'

Her face was burning once more. 'Oh. That's all right.'

'I apologise.'

'It's nothing, really. Just the same as the others, mostly.'

'Would you like another cup of coffee this afternoon? Say, four o'clock?'

Jean glanced around. Of course that would be impossible. How could he not know it would be impossible?

'There's a café on Rue Pavillon,' he said, 'just east of the park. Look for a sign with a sailing boat.'

Mary was standing on the gravel beside Miss N, who, blessedly, was yet again busy with a notebook. Georgina shielded her face and gazed up at Jean.

'I don't know if I can get away,' Jean said.

He took one stair down and turned back to her. 'Tell the others to come too, if you like.'

Miss N's fever came on quickly.

Jean had knocked on her hotel room to ask if the girls were permitted to leave their rooms to take a stroll, not quite knowing how the afternoon would play out but knowing she couldn't sit still after his last words to her. *Silas*. His name – she'd heard it only once – was like a bell.

She knocked again. But it too went unanswered and so she crept in, hoping to catch Miss N on the threshold, perhaps at work with her papers and her mind somewhere else, not latching on to the sound of the door. Miss N's room had a tall dresser with a glass dish and two blue books with titles in French, a chipped mirror with a shelf for brushes and a cup, a view of the tops of ships in the Marseilles port from the square window. But instead, Jean caught the shape of Miss N in bed and she felt a creep of embarrassment. The great woman was reduced to her mammalian mass under the covers, vulnerable, unaware. The intimacy of being in a room while another person slept – this too was in her future. The train that had brought them to Marseilles was long gone and the ship that would take them to Constantinople, tomorrow, was surely already docked at the port. Across the gleaming water, Scutari was edging closer.

'Miss Nightingale?' Jean whispered.

The word *Scutari* in her chest: it evoked music; it made her think of a wooden guitar and a man strumming it. It made her think of Silas. *Scutari*: the word was barely there. It was thin like a surgeon's blade.

What if she hated the place? How could she leave and find her way home? Or could she love the place? Another mystery. Jean recalled the nurse Irene – a girl of her nature could love anything. Irene was like a little wagon, with no mind of its own. It enjoyed whatever path it was on.

'Miss Nightingale, are you awake?' She stepped forward. Miss N's bags were open on the wooden floor and a Derry wrapper spilt out of one. Jean would have expected it to be hung on the rod in Miss N's wardrobe. All her remarks about neatness during that first leg of the journey. Exactitude in everything.

Jean listened for more sounds.

'Miss Nightingale? It's Miss Frawley.'

Jean pictured Cora and the others waiting for her to come back with an answer. They'd not made any real plans but felt the need to explore the city at least once. They could write home and say they'd been here – they would need something to say they'd done or seen or eaten or kissed.

(That was Catherine's joke. Not a woman among them thought Miss N would stand for that. In this way Miss N was like a spinster aunt, though not yet thirty-five years old herself.) Jean had left four of the girls waiting downstairs, wrappers and coats and shawls being draped on, coming off, no firm decisions. Probably out for the icy afternoon and back to the hotel in less than an hour – even the bravest among them thought that. As she waited in the still room, Jean contemplated leaving without asking and then lying: *Yes, good news! Miss N said we could go!*

'Who is that?'

Use a clear, firm voice so the patient hears you the first time.

'It's Miss Frawley. I was hoping to speak with you briefly – a request.'

Jean now stood at the side of the bed. She was so close she could see the skin, sagging slightly in places, around Miss N's neck. She had a striking face, even in sleep, with smooth cheeks and arched eyebrows, although puffy under the eyes. Her forehead was high and pale – a rich lady's face. Benjamin's sweet stepmother, Mrs Orla Turner, again came to mind: a great beauty with a face to remark upon. Jean felt a desire to reach out and touch Miss N's hair. But she restrained herself.

It was only then that Jean saw it: the sheet was twisted up under her left armpit, and sweat had moistened the hem. Jean hovered a hand above Miss N's forehead and the heat came up to meet it.

In Marseilles you can rest was what Miss N had told the nurses yesterday when they were nearing the train station.

Miss N opened one eye at Jean.

'Miss Nightingale, let me help you.'

She closed her eye, a fish in the dark.

Jean glanced back across the room to where the lantern set flickering patterns against the door.

In her old life with the Turners, Jean would have sprung into action, stripping off Benjamin's socks and replacing them with ones soaked in cool water. She could coax Anna into a lukewarm bath. The obstinate girl became mellow and weak during rare moments of illness. Jean felt struck down yet again with loss. What she'd come to think of as *heartfall* – each memory making her feel as though her heart dropped a dash in its cavity.

But she shook away those images of illness and turned to the one in front of her. Jean leant over and fussed with the blanket: Miss N now like a horse who might be startled. This would change how the other nurses thought of her. They'd want to rush to help and prove themselves. Jean hadn't yet been sure who this woman was. Their few conversations on the ship and the glimpses of her constantly taking notes had filled in some edges. But this changed things.

As if reading her mind, Miss N spoke up, seemingly composed. 'You are not to tell the others. Bring me some tea and fruit – leave it on the table – then check on me tomorrow. Leave the door unlocked. Come in early before daybreak, just you. I'm certain to be fine.'

Jean straightened up. 'Of course, yes. I'm sorry you're unwell.'

Beneath that, though, hidden like silk lining, was the thought: *I am free to see Silas.*

Here was the place. The sun was shining. A cold breeze whipped itself around her. She didn't shiver.

A few hours of freedom for Jean after she'd moved through Miss N's room with vigour, keeping up a gentle rhythm of command and control she'd come to think was the correct pace for a nurse. She laid out hot tea and a spoon on a saucer. A glass of water and a dish of porridge and sliced apple. Jean watched Miss N sleep on. Outside the dim room, her illness was still a secret. Before she'd set sail, Jean had packed into her luggage the cloth bundle containing her Gemrig rib-shears, her Gemrig gum lancet. Martin's plain scalpel. Bellocq's silver cannula. All treasured, never used. She stood above Miss N and held those instruments in her mind.

She went downstairs, set her face and told the other nurses that the answer was no. Some grumbled and closed their doors. Jean knew one or two would venture out regardless and she hoped they'd have the sense to scatter in different directions. In her own room she washed, cleaned her teeth, pinched her cheeks, took down her warmest coat, then left the hotel to find the café on Rue Pavillon. Above a skinny stone footpath, she saw the sign with the sailing boat. But the café was not open. In its doorway, between the walls of a pharmacy and a shut-up atelier, she made herself small. Invisible to everyone except for one man.

On a gust of air coming down the narrow street were the scents of the port. It was fish, it was coal, it was brine, it was the soaked-through timber of the decks. Yesterday, in this exotic place, she and Cora began calling the horses *French horses* and it had made them both laugh, the idea that a horse would know it was a horse, the idea it would understand its country of birth and the flag it lived under. Cora was pale with skin that flared up the moment she laughed or got embarrassed, as she had when she'd spilt water down the front of her dress at dinner the first night on the ship. Cora had more nursing experience than Jean, and Jean was eager to stay close and learn as much as possible. Without needing to say it, they knew that one day soon they'd be caring for soldiers who might have come off their horses, whose animals might have died right beneath them.

So she studied the French horses going by. One, then two, then three. Their glossy bodies hid all that muscle and fat, those bones and teeth inside. They clip-clopped on the stones. Their riders were men who paid no attention to her, hidden and breathless in the shadow of the doorframe, waiting for Silas.

Again, it was hunger she felt.

When he arrived, she was relieved to see his serious and searching eyes, his dark brown hair parted to the side and curling over his ears. She felt her chest expand and her eyes widen to take him in.

'Mr Bradley, hello. The café is closed.'

He touched her on the sleeve. 'Oh, I'm sorry. They keep strange hours here.'

'No matter. Would you like to take a walk?'

'Just you then.'

She held out her arm. 'Just me.' She knew she hadn't made an error. He was not disappointed. She breathed out. 'I wasn't sure you would come.' It sounded pitiful the moment she said it. She wasn't deficient; there was nothing wrong with her. But he inspired truthfulness.

'What I mean is,' she said, 'I didn't know if I should come.'

'Of course you should,' he said.

No horses went by and nobody came from the shut-up shops.

They walked west through a garden – Jean wondered what the smells would be like in spring and summer, how alive with bees and butterflies the hedges would be. She wondered how it would be possible to feel more alive than she did at this very moment. A group of children kicked a ball between them and a woman pushed a baby in a carriage at an alarming pace, weaving between pedestrians and blond-haired boys.

Silas walked with his arms behind his back, no hurry to any of his movements, and in his gentleness he reminded Jean of her grandfather the few times she'd met him as a child. Chest out. An impression of sadness that might or might not have been real. He'd been a diminutive man who tended to search for a way out of social engagements with other adults, often found down in the meadow with the children and the lambs.

'Have you been a nurse for long?'

'Less than a year.' Not a complete lie. 'The others probably have more experience than I do.'

'Miss Nightingale seems eager to teach you all and eager to get there.'

No walking outside alone.

No flowers in our bonnets. No ribbons.

No gifts from the soldiers. No excessive drink.

We will rise early, and at all times show forbearance towards our fellow nurses.

'Do you know how quickly they put us all together? Just thirty-eight nurses.'

'I thought there'd be more,' he said.

'So did I.' She liked the way he did not turn his head to listen to her – she was afraid of going red – but kept his face down and peered up, briefly, to glance at her.

She longed to touch him. She loved his broad sturdy

chest and dark eyes that were neither confident nor weak. *Clear-eyed.* He was staring across the gravel pathway, past the poplars to the stone buildings. He was looking truthfully out to the world – Jean could imagine he'd been doing that his whole life. She'd been missing touch – there'd not been any since Anna and Benjamin. Then today with Miss N ill in bed. Jean liked to think Miss N had been pleased with her lightness and discretion. She was in Marseilles. She mustn't forget it. Rose at the boarding house would demand to know what it was like, and Jean knew she must try to find time to write a letter. Time was belting on, and tomorrow afternoon Jean would be on the ship and Silas would be homeward bound.

'Perhaps I'll see you in London,' Jean said. *Perhaps I could hide from Miss N and flee the job I have not yet started and stay in Marseilles with you.*

'I thought that too,' he said. 'The odd thing is that I cannot picture it.'

'You won't want to?'

'No, I simply can't get my mind to imagine what it would be like. In London, I mean.'

A thread of nerves spun itself through her, and the only way through was to be bold. She reached up for his cheek and brushed her thumb across his eyelids. They fluttered closed at her touch. Her fingers were freezing inside her gloves. Jean swallowed and shielded her eyes from the sun. She realised how close she was to crying.

'I won't be there forever,' she said. 'Look at you – you got out.'

'It won't be a holiday.'

She stopped, and so did he. 'Mr Bradley, I know that.'

'Please call me Silas. It'd be nice to hear my name.'

'All right,' she said. 'Silas.'

'I don't know when I'll be back.'

Jean turned to face him directly. 'Well, Mr Bradley, it was a pleasure to meet you. Thank you for the information you shared about your experiences. I wish you all the very best.'

She held out a hand, the way Miss N had in the café. His eyes were so sad. Slowly, he took it, this formal handshake, and yet she felt such desire for him, through him, from him. To have his skin on hers.

Even though she had started this goodbye, Jean sought a reason to stay. One moment longer.

'I didn't have Miss Nightingale's permission to come. She is unwell – a slight fever. I helped her for a short time and now she's resting. She didn't want me to stay.'

'And she doesn't know you're here?'

Jean shook her head.

He took a step closer and one of his legs brushed against the fabric of her dress. 'I knew girls like you back home.'

She let out a short laugh. 'Charming girls? Sneaks? Liars?'

He smiled properly now, his shock like a sting across his face. 'Bold girls, Miss Frawley.'

'Call me Jean.'

'Jean.'

She caught that brass ring again – or was it gold? – shining from his little finger. 'What happened to those girls back home? Are they still there?'

His eyes shifted to the space over her shoulder.

'Silas?'

'I lied,' he said. 'There were no girls like you.'

Afterwards (it was all afterwards, her whole life was afterwards) Jean felt newly born. She must hold on to every step, to reach for it when she needed to. Remember how she got there: in a dim room above a public house in Marseilles, on a bed with a man new to her, her shawl on the back of his chair.

This was how one might cure a broken heart. (Benjamin coming down the stairs, Benjamin with his fingers in his mouth before dinner, Benjamin pulling the shells out of his curiosity box and fitting them one at a time against his cheek.)

They had left the garden, talking less and less with each block. To speak would break it; to speak would bring up the time of day and the powerful pull of bonds. Jean wanted to rinse Miss N from her mind. She had never met a Miss Nightingale, didn't know a Cora or Georgina or Irene or Mary. She didn't know the word *Scutari*, had never heard of any wars. There were no girls, no carpet bag back in her hotel room (pretend there was no hotel room). No likelihood that she might soon be boarding one of these ships down on the water (she had never known a ship).

Silas knew the way. And somehow, it seemed to Jean, so did she, propelled by desire and the locomotion of his legs beside hers while they walked. Down towards the docks and the men with buckets and crates to load and unload, and into the alleys behind. It pulsed with life. Water all around and strong men hauling crates and ropes, their bodies in motion.

'Just along here,' he said, as though he were taking her to visit the theatre. As though a chaperone might be close behind.

Silas had a room, far away from Miss N and the thirty-seven other nurses who were doing as they were told. This time tomorrow Jean wouldn't even be on land. She must keep going. They entered the public house together and inside the door was a staircase angling up to the left, peeling blue wallpaper and a brass umbrella stand in the shape of a whale. As Jean took a moment, distracting herself with how the whale seemed to be diving towards the floor, a chorus of men's voices went up in the room beyond – the tide of laughter going in then out. An invisible lone voice prevailed, hammering home a point in French that she could not understand. Jean noted how hidden they were. Nobody knew she was here – she resisted, too, the threat of this idea (Silas was trustworthy. How much she wanted him.

How *sad* he appeared to her). Curiously, Mr Turner came to mind; she imagined that the pain he had for his dead son now permeated that big house. But she also pictured him perched nearby, imparting his disappointment and disapproval of the situation she was in. She realised that all along Mr Turner had felt like a father to her. He couldn't have been more than ten years older.

Jean welcomed the other jolt, the excitement. *Nobody knew she was here.*

Silas was suddenly nervous. His voice was low. He presented Jean with a key. 'Perhaps you could go up first. Number four.'

If she said a word, the spell would break. She reached for the key and turned away and went up the stairs. Her skirt rustled on the balustrades but nobody emerged and she unlocked the door unseen. She let the door sit against the jamb, not fully closing. She breathed in the room, and her fondness for what little she knew of Silas returned in a rush across her chest. Of course his bed was neat and his bag was zipped tightly and a second hat sat smartly on top. The same blue wallpaper as downstairs was repeated up here but the effect was to dim the room. A desk sat beneath a narrow window where a notebook and pen were laid parallel. She touched the notebook's red cover and (sneak, liar) wanted so badly to open it. But she waited, first on the chair beside the desk, then she stood at the end of the bed. But that made her think too much of the way a nurse's body was alert with observation while a patient slept in her care. So she took off her shoes and faced the door in her stockinged feet.

Minutes passed.

He knocked lightly at the same time as he entered. She met his flushed face with her own.

'Jean.'

'Where are you going from here?' Jean asked. 'When you leave Marseilles, will you go back home?'

He took off his coat. 'I think that's all I can do now. I've been asked to meet Miss Nightingale, and now my ticket says I must leave.'

So they would be thrust in opposite directions.

She pointed towards the door. He kept his eyes on her and shut it.

Then his hand with its gold ring – and she didn't ask where the ring had come from, or from whom – was at her cheek and they could touch and be eye to eye, and now she recognised that actually they were almost the same height, could see that they were almost perfect together. Her body, perhaps recalling the journey over water, swayed a little. They laced fingers at their sides and kissed – she had been thinking about the ring and perhaps that was the reason he seemed to taste metallic on her tongue. She wanted to know that the door was completely shut, and couldn't stop worrying about that. She wondered how she would get back to the hotel without being caught on the stairs. The light from the window – fading now and only a matter of time before Miss N awoke with her mind intact once more.

He reached for her waist. Jean leant in to kiss him on the throat and with a hand on the back of his neck (that soft dark hair, his precious and beautiful head, the way touch felt so good again) she urged his face down to the dip beneath her ear and he kissed her there.

Jean held on, stepping backwards towards the bed. Silas held on.

In a space in her body far away from the desire she was feeling for Silas, she found herself addressing Mr Turner. *Please understand. The time I thought was carefree was the time I spent among your family, caring for two dear children in the loveliest house on the street. That turned out to be full of misery. Shock of the worst kind. Why shouldn't I spy an ad seeking ladies to nurse the sick and wounded? Why shouldn't I follow an unknown man to his room and let him undress me without the other girls noticing I was gone?*

His eyes were closed so Jean asked the question. 'Do you think, after everything, you will be all right?'

'Yes.' Silas opened his eyes. 'And you? Please be safe. Don't get sick.'

She never thought she might.

'I need you to eat well,' he said. 'Stay warm. Wear stockings – do you have plenty of stockings?'

Put your hands on me.

Jean stepped back again, and this time it was that easy – he went with her. She let him lower her to the bed. She traced a toe along his leg.

'Plenty of stockings.'

He gripped one of her feet and she noticed again the tension and life in his knuckles, in the sinewy veins. He was studying her, wanting to say more, she knew. He was going to be fine. She would see him again, she was sure of it.

Silas said, 'You'll be fine then.'

Jean's heart thumped; her blood ran. She thought of the men on the docks with the ropes at their feet. She closed her eyes. 'When we're both back home,' she said, 'come and find me. I can picture it so you don't have to.'

The passage of the ship was at sunset and Jean felt electrified, cheated that she had to leave. She'd let her room go at Mrs McLean's boarding house back in London, but had given Silas that address when they parted – surely that place would still be standing in one hundred years, with Mrs McLean inside, polishing at plates with her heavy, doughy arms. After Jean passed it to him – a scrawl on the back of a list she found on his dresser – he'd torn a neat page from the red notebook and written in tight letters his own address in Beaconsfield. Feeling despair on the ship and all she had to do was stroke this paper in her pocket and envisage this reunion – on the stairs at Mrs McLean's, on a street in his town. It gave her pause to think how she was starting to forget the Turners' house in Marylebone, ever so slightly. The memories were not so persistent, and they faded over the ocean as the *Vectis* made them all seasick once more, then as the ferry crossed the Bosphorus and neared Scutari. Soon she and Miss N and the others were plunged so quickly into their new life that the Jean who'd been with Silas in Marseilles felt like weeks ago.

She was buoyed. She was terrified. She emitted fear when packs of porters came and took their cases. Clumsy with fright, Jean tried three times to raise herself from the ferry into the carriage. All around her urgency, anonymity, misery in the eyes of the porters. Off the ferry and up the cliffs to the hospital (she noted the chill air and the sinister-looking strait when she turned back to Constantinople). She was moving in a surge, a wave, and none of these people cared if she'd made the wrong decision, or the right decision but for the wrong reasons. Why was she here? Nobody would listen to her now.

Lurching up a hill, the carriage hit something on the ground and Jean was belted into the window frame, shoulder first. She glanced at Mary and Catherine, and the girls named Kitty and Alice, but they had known to hold on tightly. They stared at her but said nothing – Jean was sure in Marseilles they would have shown kindness. She was a bag of bones, weak and insignificant as they bounced along. On top of the cliffs now they followed a wide gravel path.

She saw huts with red roofs, poplar trees, white walls, and she thought, *This doesn't seem so bad.* Tears came to her eyes and her shoulder burnt but she didn't touch it. Silas had kissed that shoulder. She sank into the seat and occupied herself with the business of keeping warm.

She had told Miss N she could do this and so she must, for as long as possible, and then she would find her way home. While she was here, she might save the life of somebody like Silas.

She softened towards the other nurses and the silence they'd brought to the carriage – Jean realised they were utterly afraid themselves, though trying to hide it. Steeliness was required in this new place. They had all intuited this.

Seeing the hospital looming in the near distance loosened their tongues. 'There it is,' Mary and Catherine said to themselves.

'Oh, it's enormous!' Alice said.

To Jean, it was as if a palace had risen before them. The hospital was high on the cliffs, built on a stone foundation. It was a vast square building with towers and spires on the corners. Row after row of windows blurred past until Jean's tears threatened again. The outer walls with their neat windows – several storeys of them – seemed endless.

At the entrance Jean exited the carriage before the others and took her bag and wrapped her cloak tighter. To her left she sensed Miss N unbending herself and stepping onto the earth.

'This way, ladies. I've received word that we have four hundred patients arriving this afternoon.'

Jean followed a porter in a long line that wound up the stairs.

'Not so bad,' Mary whispered.

'Not at all,' Jean replied.

Jean had imagined that the battlefields would be right outside their doors, chaos all around (silly girl and glad she'd kept that nonsense to herself), but, no, this seemed peaceful and ordered. A huge, tidy camp with trees and huts and dogs in the distance, open-mouthed and toying with one another's faces in the way of puppies. She soon learnt that the wretched soldiers came with their battlefield injuries at a distance of hours and days away, enduring a ship's journey, perhaps a stretcher, a wagon, a mule. Nobody to help their suffering on the way except for those less invalid soldiers who could be tasked with their care.

Jean swivelled and saw the distance they'd travelled in the carriage across the top of the cliffs that dipped down to the water – she could no longer see the port where the ship had docked. The nurses' room at the top of the tower was clean and mostly bare, and Jean set her suitcases upon the floor.

Well, they were all going to get in trouble if they did anything to a patient without a doctor's orders. They might even be dismissed back to England, having only just arrived, having barely unpacked. A stand-off emerged between Miss Nightingale and the doctors about who was there to do what. So, for three nights and four days, Jean and the other nurses sat in their quarters making bandages. A girl named Isabel sat beside her. She was tall and stooped with a mole on her top lip that waggled when she talked. In this foreign place, she seemed to vibrate with fear and excitement in equal measure.

'Where are you from?'

'London,' Jean said. 'I lived in Holborn. I was a governess.' She hoped to get it all out before Isabel could ask any specifics: did she like it, what were their names, where were they now?

'What about you?' she asked Isabel.

'My family lives in Watford. Have you ever been?'

Jean shook her head.

Isabel said, 'I've been taking care of patients since I was a girl. I used to put all sorts of animals in boxes and line them up as if they were in bed. Dead sparrows and newts. Caterpillars.'

Jean licked her lips in the same spot where the mole on Isabel's face sat. She sensed that Isabel had told this story many times before and it made Jean feel sorry for her.

Making those bandages: of course it was time spent where she could turn over in her mind what she had done in Marseilles – if they were to watch Jean, none of the girls would know that she wasn't thinking about ventilation, sanitation, cleanliness. All that repetitive cutting, tearing and rolling, the fabric through her fingers then looped into rolls, it calmed her. Movement hid how she was buzzing inside as she daydreamed about her time with Silas. She observed the way some of the girls cut and rolled slowly and delicately, and she liked that. And she also liked how others such as Kitty, with the square brown teeth and taut bun, waited for the moment to swoop in on a pile and attack strips into messy rolls before carrying them away to order into boxes.

Hours were passed in this way. Once or twice a civilian came in for treatment – a Turkish farmer had thrown his axe down towards the woodblock at the end of the day, but missed, and sliced through his big toe. They gathered around. Lengthwise, it reminded Jean of a half-eaten sausage, and she was one of the first to help. But other than these brief moments, her brain was nothing but the blooming white vacancy of sheets and towels, and talk of home. She knew other tensions were going on, with Miss N and important army officers. Jean got a sense of their short, sharp conversations outside in the hall.

The view from the hospital, which overlooked the skinny Bosphorus Strait then down to Constantinople, was a sparkling one. Minarets struck up into the sky and domes rose like half-planets among the city's tiled roofs and sunbaked walls. Jean wanted to please Miss Nightingale, and so she didn't speak much. She certainly hadn't nursed a patient yet.

Miss N also seemed to like the view. In those first days she was always coming and going to meetings, bustling about in her smooth and contained way, but would stop to stand and stare at the strait. A throwaway comment to the nurses again: she'd been to so many beautiful places. Jean listened, again, holding yet another bandage and laying it down on her pile.

Ghastly. This new world. But of course: what had she expected? This was *war*. The voice of the tailor in the shop in London, selling her the bonnet and cloak, flew to her. He hadn't told her, *War is no place for women*, which was to be expected. Instead he snipped at a loose thread with heavy black scissors and said: *Women can't imagine that sort of suffering.*

Whimpering men lay on stuffed sacks on every side of every corridor, keeping company with the rats, the roaches, the maggots. The man who was due to have an operation tomorrow might witness and hear the operation on another poor fellow today, following the path of the surgeon's knife in his own tender, waiting mind. Lice, thick as snow, swarmed over men's scalps. Help from Jean and Isabel and Louise and Cora. And Georgina – after once again falling ill on the *Vectis* – was now positively hearty, strong, lively. They were met with excrement and the fever pulsing from one soldier and the violent odour coming from another man's genitals before he could be persuaded to bathe for the first time in two months. And for a time the hospital had only hip baths. No basins, no towels, no soap. Loads of supplies had sunk into the Black Sea after a hurricane tore dozens of ships apart; it had even blown away soldiers' tents while they were inside. During winter, dysentery spread. Frostbite and scurvy took their toll.

Miss Nightingale could be found doing her patrols at night, stepping over rotten wood and the broken tiles on the floor, carrying a paper lantern purchased from the markets in Constantinople. (To Jean the lantern resembled a pet being carried around. She imagined Miss N holding the bright white lamp to her face and speaking to it.) These weren't medical calls – the doctors and orderlies did those. In the beginning Miss N was the only woman permitted inside the wards at night. The rest kept to their quarters while she saw to the patients' cleanliness and hunger, their fresh air. Miss N made plans to fix the wood and the tiles. She doled out a little wine and brandy, along with firm, clear words of assurance. She sat vigil. They were her children, she told Jean.

They sank gently, or they thrashed about, or moaned and wailed. Some soldiers ended up comforting the nurses themselves in the moments before they died. Often, Miss N needed somebody to write letters home to the wives and mothers ('You tell them he passed away bravely and peacefully. You tell them he was cared for'). Every week or so Jean got to shut herself away from the horrors of the wards to face the square of paper and summon the dead man to spin a brief, perhaps elaborate, tale.

Dear Mrs Moresby – I am grieved to inform you that your husband died in hospital two days ago. He had survived bouts of ongoing dysentery, but took a bad turn on Sunday, and became weak. I do not believe he suffered in the end. He told us that you used to make a dish with pears and cream that he loved. He was kind and strong till the end. We fed him well – whatever he asked for, if we could find it. Then your husband spoke a few words in his final hours before he slipped away.

Some had spent six weeks in the trenches, no bathing. Some had their legs amputated, their eye sockets stuffed with gauze. Most had gone hungry and the nurses learnt what meagre servings of jelly or sago or arrowroot a starved man was able to take, hour by hour. They asked the girls to kiss them, to write for them, to tell them jokes, to raise one foot higher than the other. One soldier asked Jean to breathe in time with him; he said he and his mother did it as a game when he was a child. One asked Jean to relieve him of the maggots in his groin, which covered him like salt scattered on slate. She drew the water into the basin and helped him remove his undergarments, and if her voice caught in her throat at the appalling sight she merely kept up that light knock of nothing-speech to help them both.

But he too ended up in the dead house. A final glance at his face from a nurse or an orderly, before he was sewn into his sheath and taken to the huts on the cliffs in the shadow of the hospital. Jean had been to the dead house once, after a bad night when the work of getting the bodies there had become too much for the orderlies. On bad nights, the nurses barely spoke. They marked words and numbers in books. But in the end who needed those notes? Jean would surely remember their faces for the rest of her days, just as clearly as she would remember the rough white walls of the dead house, and the straw mattresses inside the tower, with their grainy scent recalling horses, when she tried to sink into sleep.

Dear Mrs Cathcart – I am grieved to inform you that your husband died in the Barrack Hospital at Scutari yesterday. He was a jovial man till the very end and made us all laugh, despite his injuries, which were not insignificant. If it is any comfort to you, please know that he was not alone. Your husband said he was glad indeed to have glimpsed Constantinople before he died in our care.

Jean could see no relief in sight. She came to learn about the claret some nurses drank in secret and she got to doing that most nights, before whispering into her pillow words to Silas that were like notations on a white page only she could understand.

Later, she would find out how much Miss N loved to watch the surgeons at work. Jean thought: *I wouldn't look away either.* One time a patient was kept waiting – it couldn't have been longer than ten or fifteen minutes – because Miss N insisted on being present but nobody could find her. And so the team of doctors halted around the patient on the stretcher until an orderly brought her up. Jean caught her scribbling in the corner of the room while the poor soldier had his arm taken off at the shoulder blade. (A measure of chloroform. A surgeon's saw. Minutes later dead, hopefully before he noticed the hideous once-piece of him gone thudding into a tub.) She was powerful, Miss N, there with her arms folded, any flinching whatsoever happening inside her frame. Her mind was a thing at work. It was unbecoming for a woman, though Jean knew she was not like other women. But this was not the place for compliments, just as it wasn't the place for elegant dresses or fine perfumes. Miss N seemed to respect Jean more than, say, Irene or Kitty. (Could a nurse be sent back to England for chewing their dinner too loudly or leaving their balled-up stockings on the floor?)

This was not the place to bring up Marseilles or any moment from their pre-Scutari world. Neither Jean nor Miss N spoke of the fever Miss N had suffered and, although Jean kept his name radiant and hidden near her heart, nobody at all mentioned Silas.

One of the orderlies found a cat – lots of orderlies did, but this one brought his inside and kept it so matter-of-factly close that it seemed impossible to suggest that the creature, fat and the colour of dishwater, should be removed. The staff had all sorts of names for him.

Jean saw the cat on a windowsill inside the entrance. The sun was setting and the air smelt of citrus. Today Jean felt clean. She'd slept well the night before. She approached gently.

'Kedi. Kedi?'

The cat flicked his tail but refused to budge.

'Pisi?' She tried again. 'Mustafa?' The cat turned his mild, pursed-up face to her. 'Oh, merhaba, Mustafa. You want a pat today?'

He returned his attention to the sunset and a stand of trees, but inclined his head towards her fingers, her knuckle on his skull. The force of the tiny bones there.

'When I'm an old woman,' Miss N said, coming up behind her.

Jean dropped her hand.

Instead of eyeing Jean, Miss N's focus was on the animal. Her face was tired but lively. 'I will have four cats, maybe five, in my house and they can keep me company in the garden and run ahead and catch lizards for me.'

'A little army of cats,' Jean said. She liked Miss N's confidence in her future. Being an old woman seemed so far away. Her thoughts opened up to Silas as an old man. The way he might sit in a garden, smiling.

Miss N rubbed Mustafa's rump and Jean sensed the animal's pleasure – and her own – as he purred.

'I like how they pop out from behind somewhere, just when you thought you were alone,' Miss N said. 'I'll have all different breeds and colours and sizes.'

She nodded to Jean then back to the cat – a gesture that said Jean should resume her own patting. She did: this time the ears.

'He likes you,' Miss N said. She flicked fur from her fingers. 'Over in Constantinople, they're everywhere. Treated like kings and queens.'

'I didn't know that.' Now the image of the dreamy, longed-for city contained a different sort of activity: sleek bodies scattering and spilling across streets. Benjamin and Anna's cat, named Bunny, was black and ferocious and forever getting pulled into hugs before escaping up and out of Benjamin's hands like oil.

Beneath Jean's touch, Mustafa crouched. He miaowed, leapt to the ground, and dashed over Miss N's boots and away, out of sight.

'Mustafa!' Jean said. 'Farewell!'

They both laughed. They watched him go.

Like the other nurses, Jean served meals and stitched the flannel shirts and scrubbed the rotten boards and walls. They gagged at the excrement overflowing from the privies and bedpans, an inch thick on the floor (there would be houses in England, Jean knew, containing more chamber pots than a single ward here). A brain-blanking, incomprehensible stench. The men without slippers, for a time without soap. The women cleaned the utensils briskly as Miss N had taught them, saying not a word about it, because it was not the patients' fault and what would words do. As the days passed and Miss N set them to work organising, cleaning, lime-washing, Jean gagged and retched a little less. She and Cora and the other girls did as they were told and remained out of the wards after half-past eight at night. While the Bosphorus glittered outside, Jean and the others ate their cold potatoes and bread and cheese, some wine with dinner (more and more each night), and slept a dozen to a room in the north-west tower.

It was normal to talk about how you couldn't sleep. Normal to have nightmares that pulled you awake after midnight, and by then it was normal to have run out of comfort and solutions while surrounded by other girls who twitched and breathed and murmured too. And so Jean might lie awake for hours till daybreak. Sometimes in her dreams, she took a knife to a stranger's leg and tied the fragile nerve endings with her fingers. She had two hands, she had three, she had seven. In her dreams, Silas drew up from the Bosphorus Strait to arrive where she was sleeping, landing between her legs, where he covered her like a wave.

A junior surgeon named Dr Hume did not send Jean away from an operation the first time, or the next. He had shiny corkscrew curls and was long-legged like a deer. It was winter, days before Christmas, and Miss N was preoccupied, furious, with the new batch of nurses who'd been sent from England without her permission, knowing there was not enough food or clothing for those already here. The army had done it anyway.

Late one afternoon Jean crept into a room where Dr Hume was at work with three other men and she stayed silent in the shadows. He was brave, exacting, cautious, quick. In her mind she ranked those qualities for a surgeon to have. But, in truth, perhaps Dr Hume lingered too long in the wound – she physically recoiled, flinching in the abdomen as though it were her body. The way Dr Hume rummaged through the man's unnatural aperture put her in mind of a foreigner searching baskets in a souk. She willed him to probe less, though she didn't know why. And anyway – no matter which surgeon – nothing seemed to make a difference for the patients who expired so often, either on the stretcher or in the hours that followed. Dysentery and typhoid and gangrene and cholera were rife, and one day the orderlies sewed forty bodies into blankets and Jean and Cora perched on the windowsill in the tower as the poor boys were carried to the dead house. A day for Jean might end this way – bodies destined for the earth despite everything the doctors and nurses had done – after serving broth, mixing brandies, cleaning up vomit, fetching hot bricks and ice bladders, finding a deck of cards lost beneath a soldier's bed, washing linens, holding a man down on his front while a doctor prised gravel from his rump, refilling cupboards with fresh cloths, reading to a patient, taking a pair for a walk, washing a neck wound, listening to the same joke over and over when she passed a patient's bed. More letters to grieving widows. Cora wrote home each week.

'I've never seen you write a letter,' Cora told Jean one night over dinner.

'Oh?' Jean said. 'Yes, sometimes. Here and there.'

After that first surgery, when Jean had crept out of the shadows for a better view, breathless and utterly alive, she felt she had to wait for Dr Hume to dismiss her, even though she reported to Miss N alone.

He left the other doctors and crossed the floor.

'You're one of Nightingale's?'

'I am.'

'What is your name?'

'Miss Frawley,' she said. 'Jean Frawley.'

'Where are you from?' He had a northerner's accent and it was reaching through time, so close to the voice of her grandfather, her mother's father.

She swallowed. 'Near Reading. Then London.'

'You can be useful in a place like his.' He stared. 'I heard some of Nightingale's other nurses were sent home drunk.'

'I'm not one for gossip.'

To her surprise, he grinned, folding his arms across his chest and moving his feet out wider. 'Facts are not gossip, though, are they?'

'Doctor, I am useful. I like being useful. But we have our limits placed upon us.' She gestured around the room. She would pick up the blood-soaked shirt and help the orderlies with the blankets and the bandages. The body that lay before them was yet to be sewn into its final sheath. During an operation Jean was forced to think of the procedure and nothing else. Her mind couldn't snag and wander. *Please say yes.*

'Is it true though?' Dr Hume asked. 'The drinking.'

Jean made a quick calculation. 'Sometimes. Yes, a few of them. I never touch the stuff.'

He brushed at nothing on his coat and eyed her. 'Others yet are too familiar with the patients. Causing all sorts of trouble.'

'I have heard, sir.'

'Why come all this way and do the wrong thing?'

'You'd have to ask them, sir.'

A spot, white, glinted in the curls near his ear. Could it be bone?

'I have a sister back home,' he said, 'not unlike you.'

She smiled and made another calculation. 'If I can help you and these men during an operation, I'd be glad to do it. I have a strong constitution and I won't say a word.' Would he infer: *not a word during the operation* or *not a word to Nightingale*?

He seemed to draw himself up taller. They were both young, but they were not equal.

'Well, Miss Frawley, find out what you're permitted to do and if I find myself without anybody to help, I'll send for you.'

Jean had first held a surgeon's blade at the Crystal Palace a few years earlier, where she'd wandered the galleries, scooping orange sherbet into her mouth. She spotted spectroscope cards, air pumps, microscopes, keys, and silver locks like sweet little mouths. She lined up to glimpse the Queen's diamond from India – quite a bit duller in the sunlight than Jean had expected. There were wind-up toys and bottles filled with leeches. Slender as a pencil, with a single lidded eye, was a brass telescope in a gilded birdcage. Mr Colt from America demonstrated his new revolver. Then a plain-looking man and a plain-looking woman caught Jean's attention as they stood behind an open case of surgical instruments. An extraordinary force guided her to ask them for the names of the things. Jean pointed to them one by one and listened when they were named.

Gemrig rib-shears.

Gemrig gum lancet.

Martin's plain scalpel.

Bellocq's silver cannula.

Pointing, stroking, barely breathing. Her proximity, finally, to these objects thrilled her. And all with the taste of sherbet on her tongue. They told her that, yes, a parcel of instruments could be hers even though she was a woman. Her money was good enough. She didn't need to explain her odd ambition to them.

Her set was secreted away in its green cloth, in the bottom of her bag in the nurses' tower. They clinked together, the shears, the lancet folded into its wooden handle, the scalpel with a smooth ivory handle, the cannula. Inside on a cloth label, stitched with silver thread: *Wilson Family, manufacturers of surgical instruments and every description of cutlery.* To the bundle she'd added the folded piece of paper Silas gave her. And now, she thought neatly, the green cloth held both her dreams.

All through the winter it snowed. Jean bought paper from the stores and started composing a letter to Anna that she never sent – halfway through she realised the poor girl didn't need to hear from her in this dire place. Knowing this, she penned this fantasy of a letter one night, not crying but enervated by sadness: *I hope you had a good Christmas and that you went to bed early on Christmas Eve*, she wrote. *I hope you found it easy to put out of your mind the spot next to the tree where your brother might have sat. I hope you ate lots of delicious pies and puddings. Think of me here with my scraps of dirty butter and our sometimes-fresh meat. I hope you didn't go to any toy stores and see the things Benjamin would have wanted to unwrap. I'm so sorry you lost your brother, Anna. I loved him and I loved you. I'm sorry but I cannot come home just yet.*

But Jean was never Benjamin's mother – even Orla Turner never was. Did Anna think of her at all anymore? Jean put the paper into the stove and went to bed while it burnt.

The next morning she was on her rounds when she noticed Dr Hume in a sick ward checking on a patient. Standing to one side, she adjusted her sash and waited.

'Dr Hume, I'd like to once again offer my assistance as you see fit.'

'So you have her permission then?' he asked.

'Of course, Doctor.'

That afternoon, he asked her to find a screen and, after she'd positioned it, Jean once again stood close, staying silent, while they prepared for surgery, and then while Dr Hume worked.

On the other side of the room, a figure entered. Jean had not seen Miss N for days now. She had her own private room in the tower where she could work in peace and receive guests. By all accounts she worked without stopping, she barely slept, barely ate. Her anger ebbed and surged, stronger and stronger, till the rage seemed to shimmer close to her like iron filings. She was no longer the light-filled woman Jean had helped in Marseilles – but that didn't mean Jean no longer liked her. She knew Miss N was trying to find a way through the nightmare they endured in the daylight hours. The army men back home were incompetent, they were tragically short-sighted, they were without imagination, they were taking up all her time. And yet she too was here now in Dr Hume's surgery. For a second Jean considered leaving but Miss N stared till she caught her eye. No nod, no movement, such that Jean couldn't tell if she was being allowed to stay or if Miss N assumed she would go. But Jean didn't.

At first the chloroform didn't take and the thick cloths that covered the man's left thigh bled red. But Jean could tell that Dr Hume trusted himself and the blades and threads around him.

When she next glanced up, Miss N had disappeared. Two days later, Jean was surprised to see the soldier recovering in bed.

Rain lashed the peninsula. In the nurses' rooms in the tower, the ceiling leaked and water seeped through the mattresses and into their pillows, their slippers, their clothes. Freezing, wet, the sourness of damp clothes – not at all the weather to open the windows but often Miss N still insisted upon it. Some days the floors appeared cleaner and the beds warmer, the rats nowhere to be found, the men better fed. Across the strait, the roofs and spires of

Constantinople were dusted with snow, as pretty as cakes. The slate-black sea puckered beneath a sky where flocks of seagulls wheeled. Jean thought of England in winter, of Silas. And not for the first time she wondered if actually, secretly, he had a girl back home and whether the two of them were together, safe, warm. (Jean wrote another letter in her mind, not trusting that a paper one would burn in the stove: *Did I imagine your kiss on my neck, your breath, your eyes on mine, our agreed silence as we moved together in that dark blue room with people in the bar downstairs?*) She should write to ask him what home was like once more. She fantasised about a safe and whole Silas – in the smart jacket and trousers he'd worn in Marseilles – knocking on the door of the tower and finding her there alone.

One morning in February, Jean woke in the roomful of other girls: nine insensate bodies. Maybe this was how it felt to have sisters – Mary and Cora and Georgina and Alice – all piled together like kittens while their clever, vigilant, restless mother cat was down the corridor in her own room. From their original quarters filled with twelve, two girls had been sent home – Dr Hume had been right about the drunkenness – and nobody had quite known what to say while they packed. Before they left for the ferry, one of the nurses hissed at Miss N's back. She had given their orders to leave.

In the quiet darkness all around, while Jean watched, the others began to stir. Repetitive to her now: removing her night shift and changing into the flannel petticoat, the plain stiff gown and apron. Across her chest she draped her sash, embroidered in red with *Scutari Hospital*. Georgina said she didn't miss her old fancy dresses and Cora agreed that she'd all but forgotten about them, thinking they seemed rather silly now. But Jean had not forgotten. She missed the gowns she used to covet in the windows on Regent Street and all of Mrs Turner's finery. She missed the way she was allowed to admire those ribbons and gloves, the beaded silks, when garments were fresh and clean and pressed, even though Jean was just the governess. (What was Mrs Turner wearing to church now that Benjamin was gone?)

Jean took up her cap, and sat down to breakfast with the others. All day she went from bed to bed. She felt the draught from the open windows and prepared hot bottles and bricks for those who called for them. A man wrapped his head in a blanket and he lay that way for six hours, refusing all comforts, till he died, Jean never having seen his face.

At nightfall when Jean and the girls should have been returning to the tower, word came that soldiers were coming, possibly two hundred of them. Many had been injured days before. They were coming ashore.

'Miss!'

It was Dr Hume, loping now through the archway of the sick ward with his stalking long legs, and curls bouncing under his cap.

'Miss?'

It was the wrong way to address Miss Nightingale. But he had his eyes on Jean.

'Come this way.'

And Miss N followed them both.

The man on the stretcher.

She knew him and she started to say as much. Instead she sent that voice inside her, seeking comfort (it had been so long since anybody had worked to comfort her).

Was it truly Silas?

His arms were slung across his chest and his hair lay across his head in dark, sweating pieces. She saw the golden ring on his smallest finger. It wasn't a fever she was having. Not a sickness or a vision like patients often had before dropping into slumber. *He* was the man on the stretcher. The same sort of blood-soaked shirt Jean had observed on countless other troops was now on Silas. She knew what a difference it made to fetch an injured man a clean shirt even if he wore it for only an hour. In her confusion she cast her eyes around for a fresh one but of course none could be found and to leave the room was impossible. Unthinkable.

Swathes of time, the turning land and the turning sea. It was all bewildering and she felt a hot dizziness overcome her. It was simply not possible that he was here and not there, that she was here and not there, on the bed where she'd left him (it had been three months, it had been three hours). Impossible that he was not in England, chest out and moving in his unhurried way, with that unmistakable tilt of his left hand to touch the air. Memories of the past three months reached her: the visions of a soldier's face in bed and then the light all gone once he was sewn into his sheath. Her own feelings of exhaustion and boredom and weeks of horror, and the stenches and sounds that rang through the barracks. What of the sound of the latch in that room with the blue wallpaper? At the time the click of the door had signalled so clear a goodbye – such a merciful thing to hear. Without it she might have flung open the door and run back to him and not to Miss Nightingale and her duty.

Her breath was coming out calmer and she had to stay like this or they would surely send her from the room.

'Silas,' she whispered. She reached for him, knowing this wasn't allowed, knowing she was on show. But he opened his eyes to her and they were sweet with recognition. Burning with fear, she found his shoulder and then she cupped the side of his head. He was clammy all over.

'You're here,' he said.

She straightened up. 'Miss Nightingale, I think it's the gentleman we met in Marseilles.'

'Which gentleman?'

'The soldier we spoke to who was on his way home.'

'In Marseilles?'

'Yes.'

'That can't be.'

'Please. It's him. I don't know how but it is.'

'Miss Frawley, quietly now.'

An orderly was cutting at Silas's shirt and Jean moved to his side. The whole world was blood.

'What happened?'

She was asking Silas but from behind her Dr Hume spoke up. 'A series of bullets. A Minié.'

So he'd been called back to this hellish kingdom, well and whole, only to be shot.

Miss N glanced over at the men. 'Dr Hume seems to want your help here. Is that correct?'

Jean nodded. Miss N looked strangely at Silas but didn't venture forward. Jean needed to keep her force inside the room.

'Please stay,' she said. Never had she spoken so openly to her teacher.

Slowly Miss N shook her head and Jean realised how easily Silas might slip away in front of them. Miss N had liked him too, Jean knew, for that brief time in the café in Marseilles. This stoic man, with his pleasant jokes about the birds outside the windows. But for Miss N it had only been an hour and Jean realised that her teacher's focus would calmly shift to the other hundred men arriving.

'So turn your attention to him,' Miss N said. 'It appears Dr Hume trusts you.'

She would be allowed to stay, then. For a long time, the

rules that had been in place at the hospital on the day she stepped ashore had been blurring.

'Please stay too, Miss Nightingale. It's him.'

'Discipline, Miss Frawley.' When she left, Dr Hume remained, plus his assistant, the orderly and Jean.

She saw the assistant running a cloth over Silas's chest, his left side. The flesh now had a sheen upon it, clean and prepared. Her mind connected the skin there with the skin she had known in Marseilles.

She recalled her dreams with the multiple hands – they were recurring dreams now. She was capable; her mind would do what was needed. That was the message from those dreams.

Here some opium for Silas and a compress for Jean that was saturated in perchloride of iron. She put pressure on the bandage, then an ice bladder over the top. She knew Dr Hume preferred a quiet surgery so she asked no questions and held the cloth on Silas's chest. Dimly, she realised Dr Hume was watching her more closely than usual. But she couldn't care about that. Silas's eyes opened and closed and she stayed still in his gaze when it was upon her. She had learnt so much in three months, perhaps nothing more important than how pointless it was to talk about a man's injury or the spiculae coming through his hair while you changed his sheets. Miss N had taught her this but Jean had also learnt it for herself. Speak less, speak softly, speak about something else. She recalled how she told Benjamin a story about mermaids the day before he died, Jean chattering about the treasures he'd gathered on the beach and displayed in his cabinet.

To Silas she said, 'You're doing marvellously. You're going to be fine. Are you cold?'

'I bled a great deal on the field.'

'Yes.'

'It sort of came into me. Very lightly at first.'

Jean's fingers shook and felt heavy and foreign from the ice. 'I understand.' She had seen Minié bullets dozens of times and heard their deep clang when they hit a surgeon's silver pan.

His breathing quickened and his chest swelled beneath the compress. 'I know you.'

Jean felt movement in her heart. 'I know you too, Mr Bradley.'

'So you are indeed all right. I told you to be safe, didn't I.'

She brushed his forehead and leant in to whisper. 'And here I am. Keeping myself alive.'

Dr Hume's assistant came round to check Silas's pulse on one wrist and Jean placed two fingers to his neck, feeling its too-fast rhythm there, ignoring the doctor's stares. *A pulse,* she thought, *am I not allowed to check a patient's pulse?*

The sweat seemed to be coming off him in sheets. Her white apron was ruined with his blood.

'I've been thinking of you,' he said.

Jean took a cloth from her apron and patted him across his head and cheeks – she needed to hear every word, quietly, ignoring the others. This patting, anyway, was what the doctors thought the nurses did all day long.

'The chances of seeing you here …' he began.

'Silas.' She shook her head, trying to smile but panicking instead. She whispered, 'No chance.'

He moaned. Elsewhere in the hospital the same sounds could no doubt be heard. But they'd been hidden to her, all else invisible. He whispered, 'I hope I get a chance to tell you I love you.'

Dr Hume's assistant was too close. Jean nodded and gripped Silas's hand. She sent her thoughts to him.

He said again, 'Hope so.' He was blinking so fast.

The doctors were speaking and pulling out a glass inhaler and a cloth. The unpleasant zest of chloroform filled the air.

'Thank you, Nurse,' Dr Hume said. 'You may go.'

She stepped back from Silas's body, expecting to see panic in his eyes but they were already shut. The assistant came to check beneath the compress. Jean forced herself to breathe when she saw the wound that she'd been covering. To her mind it recalled a terrible flower, a hole in a wall.

'I can stay and help.'

Dr Hume's eyes grew wide. At the table, his assistant – burly with a thin beard and even younger than Dr Hume – paused but said nothing.

'Pardon me, I believe that you cannot,' Dr Hume said. 'This isn't suitable.'

He wasn't some innocent and peaceable fawn. None of them was.

'Dr Hume, let me help, I know him.'

'It makes no difference now.'

His assistant didn't look at her when he spoke. 'Nurses have been sent home for that.'

Dr Hume fixed the glass inhaler over Silas's mouth. The doctor kept his eyes on Jean till she left the room.

In the passageway she held one shaking hand in the other. In the wards, the lanterns cast murky shadows on the walls. Men were being brought in on litters and lowered into beds. Clean sheets were whipped around them like white petals, and with the new bodies arriving the windows were opened further onto the chill sea air. A mockery to think of the plans she had lined up somewhere in her mind to find Silas back in England. So much depended on that and it was all about to be taken away. In the dark, illuminated by a lamp, was the figure of Miss N – she seemed so much older than when they'd set sail in October. Her eyes were tired. Despite her height, Miss N appeared to Jean puny and frightened.

Nurses have been sent home for that. He was correct but who was left? Civilian doctors were falling ill or dying or resigning and heading back to London and Manchester and Edinburgh, here one day and gone the next.

Nobody had ever told Jean she was clever, but she knew she was bold.

She found a basin and washed, then returned to the tower and left her bloodied apron in the basket. She remembered the room in Marseilles and how Silas's gentleness and gruffness had come to life in there. She plucked a new apron from her trunk and tied it around her waist. At the sight of the stars outside the window, she felt a jolt, a desire. Down the long corridor, she piloted herself between the beds of these other men. She felt her sympathy for them springing forth, the misery of this place, that Silas should be back here. No sign of Miss Nightingale.

Hurrying back into the operating room, Jean recognised the glass inhaler discarded on a stool and Silas's body beneath Dr Hume, totally still. And in the shadows of the other side of the room stood Miss N.

There was fluid near his heart – that's what she heard them say – the wrong amount, in the wrong place. That word: *fluid*. She knew what she had felt in the pulse against his throat, whispering the count aloud to better remember it. That's what she heard and felt but what confronted her was the left side of Silas cut open. These doctors and their knives and she was glad to have missed the sinister saw at work on his flesh. She'd told Dr Hume she had the stomach for it, but she'd meant other men, other bodies. Silas's naked side in bed – she had run her palms across that skin. Exposed now were his ribs (tongue-pink, bacon-pink, brick-red, yellow) to the air (putrefaction in the air would cause disease, Miss N often reminding them about the danger of particles). A hole in the left side of his chest.

Fragile. Coming apart at the seams. Before Scutari none of them could've seen a body like this. The books she'd read and the diagrams she'd pored over now seemed the drawings of a child.

'Silas.' Jean folded her arms to keep herself in one piece, a shiver coming down from the top of her head. Her arms and chest tingled. Not able to slow her breathing, not able to breathe at all, she tucked her arms away and felt them tremble against her sides.

Miss N saw her but said nothing. Everybody knew the grudges she could hold. Jean had done right by her, hadn't she? Before they arrived, Miss N couldn't have known, by name, any troops in her care – except for this man. She spent hours organising, planning, writing, calculating, persuading, drawing. Those men were faceless but Silas had a name and Miss N surely felt it too.

Jean needed to sit, needed to stand, needed to lay down her dizzy head, needed to go back in time to Marseilles. They were stuck in this hellish barracks, the long-corridored kingdom of misery, on the edge of the world. Panic shook through her again. Every single one of them was barbaric and out of their mind and underprepared to care for a person like Silas.

She went closer. He was still. Perhaps he was breathing.

She knew chloroform was magic (she hoped and hoped it was magic). When the patients could get it, it was a marvel, a trick, a risk – sometimes they never woke up.

Inside: a glistening in his chest cavity.

Voices rushed around the room and Dr Hume began to discard his scalpels and dishes. *The word Scutari was like a surgeon's blade.*

'What's happened?'

Dr Hume turned to Jean. Miss N took one step towards them. The doctor must have known Jean had come back because there was no surprise in his face. He was weary.

Jean rushed to Silas and the other men fell away. She knew what they saw: a foolish thing rustling in her black dress and apron. Those two nurses dismissed for drinking had their favourites at Scutari and the doctors thought them weak. You could keep a favourite fellow with brandy from the stores; you could even kiss their faces when the wards were busy and Miss N was far away.

They were all far away now. Silas's chest was blood-slick, glassy with life, open to the air in its terrifying condition. His last words: *Hope so.*

And so, fast as a thief, she reached one hand in and pressed on his heart.

Dr Hume went silent. In two paces the assistant was next to Jean, smacking her away from the fragile, wet, lovely thing inside. A swift slap. A naughty girl. Some words from the doctor on Silas's right side, but he didn't meet her eye. And then the room was still. The man at the centre, their brief star of the show, had died.

It was a whirring, strung-out Miss N who took Jean by the elbow and drove her out the door. Her energy was like that of a hummingbird. They stood in an alcove. Miss N nudged her boot against a lone straw mattress shoved against the wall, and Jean could almost hear the trivial plan forming in Miss N's thoughts – how to address the problem of a mattress that should not be there. That the woman would return to her duties – of inventory, of bossing, of harassing, of nitpicking – within minutes of Silas's death filled Jean with revulsion. From inside the surgery she heard low voices, the sound of table legs against the floor, metal instruments thrown into a bowl. So chilling, also, to note the silence of Silas's body on the table. She heard the absence of him.

'Miss Frawley, what is going on?'

'I had to try something.' Jean struggled to get the words out.

'What if you killed him?'

'That was not my intention.'

'You had no business being there.'

Jean tried to keep her tone even. Hysteria wouldn't do. 'None of us has any business being anywhere.'

Miss N whispered, 'Softly, Miss Frawley, you are too loud.'

'Fine, Miss Nightingale,' Jean said. 'I'll whisper.'

They faced each other. Silence surrounded them. Jean was overwhelmed by fatigue. He was *gone!* He was barely here and now he was gone.

Tentatively, composing herself, Miss N patted Jean's arm. 'You are competent and diligent. And perhaps Dr Hume took a liking to you as well. I should have put a stop to that as it appears you've become excited by the surgeries. I blame myself.'

'Don't blame yourself. I have free will.'

Miss N withdrew her hand. 'I know that.'

'I told you it was him. I told you.' *Though what could Miss N have done?*

A sharp reply: 'These men – the surgeons – are doing their best. The soldiers – we do our best for them. Warmth, diet, comfort, kindness. For some that is all.'

'Warmth would not have saved him,' Jean said. 'It was not for a lack of warmth that he died.' The impression again of reaching in, pressing on his heart. She brought that hand closer to her face; the fingers were sticky with blood and other clear fluid. Nothing about it disgusted her.

Miss N turned soft. 'Here. Let's wash ourselves.'

Jean's arms were shuddering. 'And now he's gone.'

'Come.'

Miss N reached for her but Jean recoiled. 'No.'

'You've had a shock.' A note of frustration in the voice of the mother cat.

Jean's heart was racing. Yesterday she hadn't known he was anywhere near her: he was in the west, she was in the east. The agony of him on his stretcher, then the cart inching closer to their sprawling, lit-up barracks on the edge of the sea, and her completely unaware while she put gravy on her plate and folded up her stockings. In the background, Mary sang *Norah, dear Norah* while the girls talked about the nightmares they hoped not to have at bedtime.

Jean looked up with her eyes wide at Miss N. 'I could have saved him.'

'You might also have killed him. Silly girl. Come. Come.'

The night passed. She heard whispers among the other nurses; they knew she had suffered something – perhaps to do with news from home, perhaps to do with a man. It was not like Jean to be this way. Up in the tower they kept up the quiet singing, and one of them lowered Jean onto her pillow. Cora wet a flannel and dabbed it on Jean's temples at the pressure points. Over Christmas, Cora had been fond of a soldier but had kept it secret from everyone except Jean. As far as they knew, Miss N was oblivious. Mostly the soldiers wanted to imagine that you were their sweetheart, or their sister or mother. For some: their daughter. They wanted to know where you were from and you could either tell them the truth or make up a place you wished you were from. It was quite harmless and the good nurses, Jean thought, went along with it. What did it matter in the end, despite Miss N's warnings. Either the end was the recovered man walking out of the barracks, all thoughts of his once-sweetheart Cora gone and replaced with the dreamy love of ship and of home, or the end was the man with his head wrapped in blankets – and whatever words had been said by whichever girls by lamplight before he perished were insubstantial, less than nothing.

Cora tried to take Jean's hand but it was the one she'd touched Silas with. Washed now, but alive in a special way for her, so she tucked it under her blanket.

Georgina asked, 'Is it bad news from home? Is it a fever?'

From her own cot Alice said, 'Come on, Georgina. Look at her.' And that seemed to end it.

They expected her to doze right off. Jean knew they'd be waiting and she listened to the false, petty conversations that were on show. They would wait till tomorrow or the next day to draw out the full picture from their friend. In this splinter of the world, they could wait if the story was good. Jean stroked her chest and recalled his words: 'I hope I get a chance to tell you I love you.' It hardly mattered if he meant those words in that moment – that he loved her. She knew he thought he did. Maybe what he meant was: *I hope we have time to get to know each other, because I know I'll come to love you.*

Jean pretended to fall asleep and heard the others washing, undressing, sighing, retiring for the night. Inside, something was coursing through her, keeping her more awake than ever.

She had not visited the dead house alone before.

Jean rose to put on her bonnet, shawl and cloak. After she checked her sisters' sleeping faces, she eased out the door, carrying her boots. She went down the stairs and the long corridors, doing up her laces and stealing a lamp from outside the kitchen. She nodded at the few orderlies she saw – she was dutiful. With her uniform there was no mystery whose command she was under. Outside the entrance the icy air knocked into her face and chest. The lamp went out and she set it down at her feet. She raised her hood over her head and pressed its sides to her cheeks.

Down the path she went, filling her lungs with the air that stung her eyes and bit her flesh. Jean saw how the palaces and mosques glittered across the water, but they blurred as tears came spilling onto her cheeks. She'd been cheated by a love affair. It had given her hope and then all was dashed. Cheated, too, by Benjamin's death while he was in her care. She wanted to get at both of their bodies now. She wanted to understand what she might have done. From her family's Bible, a story she remembered: Jesus and the man Lazarus in the stone tomb. Jesus told the man's sisters that sickness would not end in death. If Jean's hands had a life of their own, a competence of their own – as they did in all her dreams – maybe they could bring a body back to life.

Behind her the barracks rose to the night sky. She sidled past the huts and the barren poplar trees, hoping that her black dress and cloak would make her invisible to any officers. The moon was showing half its face. For company Jean would have liked a flock of the wheeling, shrieking gulls. She and the creatures could be incomprehensible together. But no birds were about. In the distance on the cliff's edge was the cemetery, where the pale sarcophaguses were lined in rows like tablets. Others had modest wooden signs fixed to their grave sites, the mounds of fresh earth like tender sores. Each day bodies were transported to that cemetery. Till then, the soldiers lay silent in the dead house. Perhaps Miss N was at this moment writing home to the wives and mothers of today's losses. A chill ran through Jean to recall Benjamin's small body alone and unmoving, eventually relinquished from the last caress he would ever know.

She heard voices calling from the officers' huts, carried on the wind that was wracking at her side. She gathered her skirts and trotted the last bit there, sending breath through her body before she pushed open the door to the dead house. The smell of putrefaction came from within but this was nothing new. She tugged her shawl up to cover her nose. The hand with which she'd touched Silas's heart was freezing. Wooden shelves the width of a man were built along the far wall and the blanketed bodies were lined up with their toes pointing towards the centre of the room. Two windows let in slivers of moonlight.

She was clear-eyed while she stood counting.

Fourteen bodies in their sheaths.

So it had been a quiet day, then. A short *ha* tore up from her gut and echoed against the walls. That Silas should be part of a contingent of hundreds of men arriving across the Black Sea in those hours, but that only he and thirteen others should perish. A grotesque and unhappy thought.

The only pleasing thought: not many bodies and one of them was Silas's.

Where to start?

A man's voice called out, 'Hello?'

She tucked herself in the shadow of the door where the moonlight could not reach.

'Sir?' The voice again. 'Hello? Is somebody there?'

Swinging through the gloom – she had not known there was another room, connected through an internal door – came an orderly in blue jacket and trousers. He was holding up a lamp. He was tall and skinny with sharp features and a thin red beard – a youth. He had a stealthy, low energy. A creature used to the dark.

His voice was closer now. 'Wilkinson, is that you?'

Behind her shawl, Jean held her breath and tried to halt her trembling. The man's lantern was casting shadows that moved like the wings of bats across the ceiling and walls. In the brief seconds of brightness when his swinging light met the wrapped-up bodies, Jean tried to intuit which was Silas's. Impossible. If she could just have ten minutes. Ten minutes and she could find him once more. Why couldn't she have just a moment?

Underneath that fiery, quick-blood feeling: fatigue was pulling at her and yesterday felt so distant. She should have known somebody would be at the dead house to keep watch. She'd read stories in the newspapers of wretched people waking up. Catherine and Irene were known to murmur their prayers at the sight of a sheath on a wagon; Catherine insisted she'd known a priest who had known another priest who once discovered a dead body still alive.

The orderly's footfalls rocked across the wooden floor. And then they were face to face. 'Oh, God, blazes, I see you.'

Jean shut her eyes. The desire to dash out from the doorframe and flee, unrecognisable surely at this time of night, running up the path and across the cold cliffs to the hospital. But in the coming hours the story of this event would widen like a net over the other nurses while officers searched for a culprit. No, she couldn't include them in any hunt. For one, it was wrong. For another, she was tired, so tired. And a calculation: it had only been a few months. She wasn't sure the loyalty of her fellow nurses would hold.

'What's your name? What are you doing here?'

'Miss Nightingale sent me.'

'She *sent* you?'

'Sir,' Jean started. 'I—'

'What's your name? It's after midnight.'

'I came to check on the body of a man.'

He was so close he could have seized her arm. She'd never seen him before but no matter: they were all the same (he to her, she to him). It was an unusual relationship between the lowly nurses and the lowly orderlies. Coming from all over England, many of them were mere boys.

'What for?'

'We knew him,' Jean said.

'Miss, could you take down your shawl?' He wore nothing around his face and nose.

Slowly she undid the knot at the back of her head. She balled the fabric into a pocket in her cloak. 'I said: we knew him.'

He stared. He'd edged the lantern in her direction and there was no doubt he saw her properly now. 'Well, what about him?'

'I need to see the body.'

He started to speak then stopped. Finally: 'I can't let you do that.'

'She sent me.' But this time Jean's words sat differently. He knew. The lie was a stone between them; the boy might play with it now.

He whispered, 'You girls get all sorts of nonsense in your heads, don't you.'

'Would you let me?'

'Go back to bed, miss.'

She let out a sob but turned her face up to him, smiling. 'He'll be buried today, is that right?'

'Miss, that's just what happens.' The boy waited. 'I'm sorry.'

But she didn't move. 'I don't know what to tell you. I cannot leave till I see.' The bodies in their shrouds – maybe the one closest to her? Was that him?

'Miss, you've something strange in you.'

She reached out her good hand. Once more the smell of the dead wafted across and coiled itself into her. 'If I could just—'

'Stop!' he yelped, grabbing her by the arm now, staring her down.

They both tilted their heads towards the noises – shouts and footsteps, a dog barking – that were coming from outside.

She felt his fingers digging into her cold flesh as he whispered, 'I *told* you to leave.'

When she was a girl of six, maybe seven, Jean had found herself hungry, which was not unusual. Out of the house she went, alone and down the lane to the horses' stables. The horses were not theirs, and Jean kept out of the way of the boys who worked the forks into the hay, and the boys who brushed the animals' powerful brown bodies, and those whose fingers raked through the buckets of scraps. Her hunger was profound, a sizable jag through her tummy. Memories of all those other times – nights in bed when she couldn't sleep for the hollow she felt and mornings playing dully with her rag doll on the kitchen floor beneath the empty table – would later form a mass of their own. But the memory of the day with the horses stayed with her. Her back was against the stable door and she sat studying the legs of adults walking past. Her teeth felt the food in the air; she felt the grains running along her tongue, her gums, down her skinny throat, her mind crunching down.

First: she waited, giving in to the sense of hunger, knowing an end was coming soon. Second: she listened for the voices of the boys and the clunk of their forks against the wall, telling her they were done. Oh! And then she was inside. She was barely as tall as the underside of the horse, but she was smart enough to know not to approach him from behind. He eyed her – seemed to know her – and shuffled back. Jean had heard others speaking to horses and she knew to adopt this same sort of coo: *There, boy, all right, good boy.* When he took his gentle, dark eyes from her she crept towards the pails she hoped were filled with beets, turnips, apples, oats. She spied three fleshy pieces of vegetable, dashed her hand in and picked them out. She popped them on her tongue and chewed. She had a sense that the horse didn't mind, and was curious, and kind. But before she could reach in for more, the boys came back and she was caught. She was a naughty girl, they told her, and it was foul, what she was doing. Shame crashed upon her, and the spark of those chewed-up ends of carrot and apple was gone. Others had called her naughty before but these boys were gleeful about it, astonished. They didn't come after her, though, and the horse, from the corner of its stall, crushing hay beneath its hooves, seemed to tell her she could do it again.

Jean wrenched her arm from the orderly's grasp and pushed out of the dead house. She took her shawl from her pocket and twisted it around her neck to fend off the cold.

Across the paths of the barracks Jean went, not running but striding and swiping away tears from her cheeks. For a moment she paused and stared at Constantinople. She wondered at the people there and the women at work in its streets. They said it was a beautiful city, one of the most dazzling in the world. She wished she'd tried harder to cross the strait and venture into its squares and eat some golden fruit from a market. Behind her, she heard voices at the dead house but she did not turn around.

A man, sounding rather more baffled than aggressive: 'Miss!' It was a single cry out and he did not try again. She pressed on into the night. She was a solo body, a solo heart, and a force was catching up to her.

Give her an hour, the night, in peace. They would have to find her.

News travelled swiftly. Miss N didn't need spies. She was the net thrown over the hospital – yes, some things escaped, but most didn't. Hours later, before breakfast, Jean was summoned. It was a knock at her door, a message from Matron to meet Miss N in her office. It was Jean feeling utterly small as she got dressed in the room with her sister-kittens, the expectation of punishment dreadful and sure. It was fear of the final and inescapable distance this would put between her and Silas's body (oh, *Silas*; the boy in the hut keeping watch over him; the cart on its way; the soft mouth of the earth coming for him).

But it was also clarity: she had lasted three months, nearly four.

Jean knocked.

'Yes. Come in, please.'

Miss N sat at a vast desk in the centre of a room Jean had never before visited. The floorboards were scrubbed, the walls were whitewashed and vibrant green plants in pots stood beneath open windows. Behind her desk, Miss N was driving her pen backwards and forwards across a page. Jean expected her to stop writing to focus on listing Jean's crimes and punishments. But instead Miss N motioned at the two chairs that faced her and made a sharp stripe in the air with her pen. *Sit down.*

Without raising her eyes, Miss N said, 'Some days, a chilly room can be an invigorating place in which to work.'

As though she'd been poked, Jean hugged herself. She

chose the chair further away from Miss N, who seemed guarded but also buzzing. On her desk were stacks of creamy paper, red folders, jars of pens and pencils, books open and creased with force. Envelopes with torn-off ends and unopened mail were stacked together at her elbow. Miss N leant to her right and sat dead still to inspect a page. Two fingers fluttered at her lips. She wrote another line, tossed the pen into a jar and turned her full attention, finally, to Jean. There were shadows under Miss N's eyes, and Jean saw the ropy lines of tendons in her neck.

'I have had reports,' Miss N began slowly, 'that one of my nurses ventured out to the dead house last night.'

Jean found herself nodding, for longer than was normal. She couldn't stop. She couldn't speak.

Miss N clasped her hands together on the desk. 'That business yesterday with Mr Bradley was a shock. He was kind to us in Marseilles, wasn't he.'

Jean nodded again.

'I have to admit I don't remember much about him. But he was a nice man, very polite.'

'It was a shock to see him, yes.'

'Sometimes men are redeployed. Sometimes men re-enlist if the reality of home life is too great to bear.'

Jean pulsed with those few precious words she and Silas had spoken about home. The tears were coming now. 'Do they?' she croaked.

Miss N wasn't in the habit of repeating things. 'I can

therefore understand,' she went on, 'that it must have been difficult to find him in such a tremendously delicate situation.'

Jean forced the heel of her palm – one, two – quickly into each eye.

'But, Miss Frawley, that was entirely inappropriate. Doing what you did. You had no right to touch his body like that.'

Jean stiffened, not knowing how to say *his body was mine*.

'Nothing in your training before here, nothing in my training suggested what you did was appropriate behaviour for a nurse. Unnatural too. We serve the doctors at this hospital *in the manner they wish us to*.'

Jean watched herself from above, in this bright, clean room. What would become of Silas's things? He'd mentioned that both his mother and father had died. All those letters home to the wives and families of other soldiers and she'd been so careful to mention that their men had not suffered, so careful to remark on a physical feature that a loved one was sure to remember and adore.

Her own body had taken over yesterday, a reminder that she was flesh and bone and impulse. Her legs started to shake.

'You are lucky not to be investigated.'

'I had to try something,' Jean said.

Pure shock on Miss N's face and her cheeks reddening. 'You had to do nothing except what was permitted of you.'

They stared at each other.

In a whisper, Jean asked, 'Do you expect me to apologise?'

Miss N's mouth opened slightly. 'I expect my nurses to show restraint, to be obedient. I don't need apologies. But some reflection on your part would be revealing. I simply fail to understand *why*.'

'Silas's heart. I could see it.'

'Silas?'

'His name, Miss Nightingale. You know that too.'

Miss N closed her eyes and paused. 'Things – with you – could have been different.'

Jean felt the air go from her but steadied herself. *Use a clear, firm voice.* 'I have not been drinking. I have been hard-working. Attentive to my patients.'

Abruptly, Miss N leant over to get a pen, but something about the gesture struck Jean as false: she was more rattled than she wanted to let on.

'Miss Frawley.' She stabbed the air. The pen was a weapon. 'Are you fighting to stay?'

Jean shook her head, tears streaming again, thoughts of home rocking within her. 'I only did what I knew I had to do.'

'Well, I've never witnessed anything stranger in my time. Unbecoming. Risky, risky, risky.' Miss N motioned around her. The whole hospital was her domain. The whole hospital was waiting to see what she would do. 'And then this business with the dead house in the middle of the night.'

'I never said that was me.'

Miss N gave a sigh. She was tired now of playing mother, tired of toying with a child who refused to admit fault. 'That will be all, Miss Frawley. Gather your things. Matron will sort out the details of your journey home.'

She had nowhere to go, no family, couldn't face Mrs McLean and whichever innocent girls were sleeping soundly there now. Jean had not kept up her correspondence with the Turners – still ashamed by this. Not one letter! *Dear Anna* – it would have been so easy, but too much time had passed.

Halfway into her trip home, third class this time, on the steamer, she wondered if she should have headed instead for France or Germany. Continue to be unknown, and see how that rubbed against the rawness of her grief. To try to cast Silas from her mind. On the ship she avoided others as best she could. She sat alone at dinner, ate desperately at the meals prepared by the cooks. Soup, ham, peas, thick buttered bread. Fish pie, which reminded her of Mrs McLean's fish pie, and that, at least, had her standing on the deck breathing in the ocean towards home. From Folkestone it was a train, and then another. She caught sight of her past self making this journey, so quickly, in the opposite direction in October, when the voice of Benjamin was clear in her ears and her two packed cases were at her feet.

It was Rose who helped first, sending word with her new address. So Jean disembarked and made her way to a building in Southwark, where Rose stomped down the stairs of her flat in the early evening, took hold of one of Jean's cases and then waggled her fingers to make Jean give her the other. Nothing had changed, yet everything had changed. Scutari had taken a toll, she knew, and others would realise it too. She settled into the feeling of her feet on solid ground, in a flat on Frean Street after so many days at sea. She hugged her friend.

They sat at the table and had cups of tea.

'You can stay here,' Rose said.

Precisely where she could sleep, Jean did not know. But none of this was hard after what had happened. It was no different from their tiny rooms in the boarding house, Rose thinking she'd get work on a theatre stage and Jean soon to depart for her post with the Turners.

'Thank you,' Jean said, her eyes filling. The truth was she could sleep anywhere. She could sleep right now.

'Ah, any time,' Rose said. 'You can pay me in stories. Been anywhere lately?'

Jean shook off her tears. 'Can't think of a thing.'

They stopped. Enough with the jokes.

'All right,' Jean said. 'Let me tell you what it was like.'

In the meagre light of the lamp, across the table, they held hands. Events of the past year pelted Jean, image after image and sound after sound. What would she do now?

'One day at a time,' Rose said.

III

South Street, Mayfair
August 1910

Florence

The war was over. The men signed the bits of paper. And I was not in a hurry to get home. Who would have me, I wondered. And who would *I* have? If ever I thought I didn't have much in common with others back home, then leaving behind a broken scrap of Europe I truly felt like the only person on the planet. I received letters from my family and, yes, I did reply. I think they were careful to say they were eagerly awaiting my return and would help me make a home wherever I wanted it to be. But I sensed, also, that this further time apart gave them space to work out what to say when we next saw one another. I moved as though I was in a bubble.

I dreamt of returning, for good, to Marseilles, a city of peace – ships on the harbour, children gathered around fish flashing in the sunlight. Why not Marseilles, where I'd stayed with my first group of nurses? In that city we had no notion of what was in store for us. I could sit in the sun and empty my mind, all alone with my face turned to the sky. I could go for walks in the evening and survey the harmless lights on the harmless ships. And who would know me?

But of course Marseilles was only a brief stop – and Athens too – after I was put on a ship bound for England, with Lea Hurst looming ever closer. It was summer – long days of sun overhead. I wrote in those black notebooks (over there, in that box) and I slept and slept and slept.

After the war, Mother and Parthe followed me to London, while I was doing my work for the Royal Commission. My mother and my sister, who didn't always wish me goodwill. I made my own little war office at the Burlington Hotel. I walked the length of Mayfair with Parthe, her arm hooked into mine. At night in bed I prayed to God and I contemplated my evidence and my questions about a war that killed twenty thousand British soldiers. Around me, silk curtains shifted in the breeze, and in the morning the sun glinted off the silver tea service, and somebody, somewhere, was already preparing our dinner.

Just as I had before my superintendent post at Harley Street, I read the government reports, the blue books. (Reports on the living conditions of the poor in East London. The 1840 report on the Health of Towns. The 1842 report on the Sanitary Condition of the Labouring Population of Great Britain.) As a woman I couldn't sit on the commission but I worked and worked to deliver them an account of the trials I went through, endlessly, trying to get at something, like a hook from a hunter, and work it out of my flesh. Each time I thought I'd come close to solving it, to exposing mistakes and wounds, to absolving a piece of myself, to laying out what could be done to prevent the same in the future, I'd turn the page and more words poured through me. I needed to be alone to examine them all; the well was never dry. I drew up plans, analysed statistics and finessed those graphs they loved to gape at.

Endlessly I watched Mother and Parthe ready themselves at their dressing tables to go for carriage rides or a stroll around Berkeley Square. *These gloves, or this pair? This bonnet or this one?* How uncharitable to have such thoughts about them. I saw too late that Parthe had spent months seeking donations for British soldiers, and that my family's presence was a kindness – I was unwell and they kept people away from me. And if at the time I thought they were coddling me like a child, perhaps it was because my spirit at the time was that of a child. Some days I could barely eat or sleep because of my unease. Starvation, dysentery, cholera, frostbite, maggots in old wounds, fleshless bones protruding from limbs. Words would get me out of this. It was words that had got me there, made me responsible for thousands of men's lives, and for a while all I could picture was my earlier self praying to God for a way out, writing letters, scribbling in my journal, speaking, beseeching, arguing, begging, fighting – once dashing a teacup on the ground in frustration with something Mother had spoken aloud.

Why sleep when there was so much to do and all that waited for me were nightmares?

But in truth I was happy for much of it – I had vaulted over the tyranny of idleness. Never again would I simply be a rich lady stuck in a drawing room, forced to read aloud from a frivolous book, be interrupted, then start anew in another one, and be interrupted again. Or listen to a guest I didn't know read aloud from her book till a gentleman standing at a window decided it was his turn and took up his prattle.

'Miss Nightingale, how many men perished?' they asked me in the summer of 1856. London in August during the ghastly Royal Commission, with days that unravelled like bandages.

Question: *To what do you mainly ascribe the mortality in the hospitals?*

Answer: *To sanitary defects.*

It's August again now.

Images of the hospital at Scutari rise upon me on some long days – days when I haven't eaten a thing, days when I want comfort but don't think to ask Mabel for it. For they were nothing more than slaughterhouses before I arrived and I've learnt to try to plunge those images down like a kitten that I must drown in a bath. My mother and sister enjoyed my nice things and they enjoyed my fame – but they also fought on my behalf and tried to keep me safe.

My family, and the Bracebridges and Dr Sutherland and my devoted Aunt Mai and Arthur, and, oh, a few other beloved sorts that I've lost to memory, understood that the tide could turn against me at any moment. And the questions would go from 'What did you do …?' to 'Why didn't you …?' or 'How could you …?'

When Mabel first arrived at my house, here on South Street, she found those notebooks in a case beneath my bed. She asked me, *while undoing the clips right before my eyes*, if she could open the thing. Yes, I said, stunned at the new girl and her boldness. *Ooooh*, she said, or something similar. *Notebooks!*

Look, I could be buried up to my neck in my notebooks. But the one from Marseilles before I set sail for Scutari has become so special to me. I drew in it, sketching all manner of things: birds, bread, horses, the children running in their coats and hats. So it wasn't just me writing away as I've done every day since my dear father began his great and unending project in me, calling me his *only genius*. Mind you be careful with those ones, Mabel. For in those books I let my mind unspool, because Marseilles was the place where I spent that time with my young, unbroken nurses. Nobody knew who I was and I didn't yet know what Scutari had in store. In that city I had a fever and Jean tended to me (apple on my tongue, the quiet closing of the door, my skin tender and hot). And in that city I met Silas in the café. Oh, the scent on the air in Marseilles, which has remained unmatched to me. Filthy London. Even now.

So too the clean air of Malvern, the spa town where I was the patient, one year after the Crimea. They treated me with cold-water packs to cool my blood and slow my pulse. Well, whose pulse could slow after visions of my poor beloved Athena, headless! Without her claws! Athena being pecked and poked at. The high ceilings of that room in Malvern where my brain – rather than unspooling freely – sort of jagged and looped and *wept*, if it's possible to say a mind can do that. Feelings of anger (that those department men should blame *me*, as though I had been the one to build a hospital over a cesspool), of guilt (I realise that now, though certainly not at the time) – feelings of deep and abiding horror came upon me, all while I was there alone, although I know members of my family wanted to come. When Father argued his way in, I saw a strange look pass over his face, like a light going out, and he remained that way for his very short visit. I barely spoke a sentence to him. At one point he tried to get me to stand and I recalled our lessons when I was the schoolgirl and he the schoolmaster. At Malvern I must have seemed to him a stranger in face and body and manner and memory. It had all been shot out of me.

What I recovered has come back in pieces. And just imagine! When I left Turkey I was but thirty-six years old!

And a mind disintegrating slowly, in an unwell body that ought to have given my father grandchildren and be plump and motherly. But at the hospital in Malvern I sat in the chair, the door closed, his big hand encircling mine. And when I think of him now, the moments where we recited sonnets and studied composition, grammar, Latin, history, Greek – all sweet memories – wink in and out, mingling with the recollection of the two of us at Malvern, each waiting for the other to say something that would bring it all to an end.

Silas

Afterwards, when I woke up – well, I didn't really *wake* but I wasn't to learn that till later – I was lying on my back with my arms folded against my chest. A wisp of fabric made a bridge from my nose to my mouth. I sensed that I had been placed somewhere unlovingly. Darkness all around.

I cast about for a moment, saving up this second to be able to tell somebody back home. My first thought was my mother – a soft sort of comfort to confess something to a dear person who had nothing but good thoughts in their head for you your whole life and not much else besides. But my mother had been dead two years, and Pa had been dead for one, both buried in the churchyard. I was halfway around the world so our cottage at the bottom of the valley was empty. My next thoughts were for Jean. I had found her, had seen her beautiful face, if only for a moment. She was alive and well and I felt certain I would see her again.

It wasn't pain exactly, but my arms against my body had a fizz to them, as if bubbles sat right beneath the surface of my skin. *Sure enough*, I thought, *I've been asleep and the blood and muscles need waking up.* My eyes too: not adjusting, nothing coming into focus. For several moments I'd been preparing to *get up* but hadn't accomplished this. My wrists and knees, at the joints, began to ache.

The fact that all those times I'd been alive I hadn't quite realised it, not properly, considering that death is looser than you might have thought, unless you thought all along that it would be serene and nothing more than a lapse. Quick and clean.

My mind went into a sort of half-state. I was there in the hastily built dead house, the pain-filled dead house, but I was also back with my father at the stream near my house while we sat and watched the water rub its way across the black stones. I was back with Jean in the bed we shared, back with her at the café while she stirred her coffee and brought the pearl-handled spoon to her lips.

A little more life than in sleep, but less than awake.

Around me the doctors had spoken and perhaps one of them checked a timepiece and pronounced something final. The men had stayed in the room, yet somehow Jean was no longer there, and I was aware of a drumming in my brain.

I wondered why I was being covered up and not cleaned up. I wanted to know where Jean had gone.

This type of thinking would get me nowhere, I had the mind enough to think. *Don't lie there like a puppet. Think harder. Move!* Where had that pain gone – that was a more important question. Precisely where and when did it go, and did it in fact just *disappear?* Out of my fingertips or something? Because I'm sure of the bullet and all that blood. I can't have made that up. Something was telling me to sit up and talk to these men – but tell them what exactly? All the pieces hadn't fallen into place. As far as I knew they'd forgotten me and were on to the next patient already. *Wait!* A welp came from my mind. No great panic though; things were too quiet for that. No great rush. Not yet anyway.

It wasn't *breathing* that I was doing – I wouldn't have called it that. But it was an *in-out, in-out* going through me and something in me settled, still very frightened for what it all might mean.

As the years passed, I have come to think of the place where I dwell – neither dead nor alive – as the river. A bank on one side, and one on the other. And in between: shock, pain, loneliness, but also occasionally peace, and a new kind of existence.

And then I was back in my life, I was back in my story. The heart I had never spent much time imagining, never greatly thought about, had sent me back, had sent me forward. If others exist as I do, ghosts in the city and on the water, were their lives similar to mine before they were shipped off, frozen, starved, diseased, shot in the mud? What happened to me was not destiny – I don't believe that. Everything could have been different if my father hadn't died when he did, or if I hadn't boarded the ship to Turkey, or even if the horse carrying the man who shot me had startled and stumbled its hooves into a ditch, the bullet dispatched in any other direction on earth. The river, the river. Any twist or turn elsewhere and I never would have met Jean in Marseilles, that fragile stroke of luck. And where and when would I have died then? Rather than these years of wandering and trailing off, my life might have opened and shut like a book.

Instead, after the war, I had a second life where I did not age. I searched for Jean at the address she gave me but I never saw her come in or out of the house in Holborn. I roamed around, not sure how long this new life would last and not convinced others couldn't see the truth about me. I fell in love with a woman named Meg – a widow, funny, always laughing-bright, with eyes that crinkled at the edges – whose husband had been struck by a carriage and died. Her sons, William and Tom, always wanted to go on the spinning thing near Brighton Aquarium, so Meg and I took them there on Saturday mornings, late in 1890 but before winter really took hold. Meg had been having trouble with her hands – they looked fine to me, but they gave her grief. The skin, the way it was wearing away in patches. She needed a balm from somebody. She had the name of a strange woman on a scrap of paper, and I had half a mind to leave her and William and Tom on the beach and find her the ointment myself. A man can earn praise for trips like these.

True, at times I found some happiness, the days unfolding like a gift: I wondered how long it would go on. But I still cared about the life I'd had, and I yearned to be seen *properly*, for there to be an end point. And though I loved Meg, she was not Jean. Was never Jean.

I thought of Jean every day and every night.

When she walked past, her skirts kissed the ground. Standing beside me at the stretcher on that final day, her head was tilted slightly, her chin up to show she could hear me. How she had been in the room above the pub – desperate for me. I remembered it all.

After Meg there was Agnes, whose father ran a theatre troupe in Eastbourne. Leaving Meg – which is what I did, early one morning before the boys rose but when Meg was awake, staring at me from the corner of our bed – was a terrible injury. A cruel thing I did to her and to that pair of boys, who mostly faded from my memory after I left. I can't imagine what they must think of me. Agnes had no children, couldn't have them apparently, and when I caught sight of her trussed up as Cleopatra one evening through the wonky archway of the Oak and Grouse, well, most memories of Meg faded too. The river made me drift. A man is always searching for his footing.

I can't say how long it was before I figured out the special part of me.

Each morning I wake – for I still sleep, still wash my bedclothes, even though they don't need it. My joints throb and ache from sunrise to sunset. Ankles and wrists and the backs of my knees are stretched tight and hard. The soles of my feet feel as if they're being stabbed with shards of glass. And in the past few weeks (hard to say how long) I've felt myself coming out of a strange summer hibernation. The pain an agony. And still this *in-out* going through me: I haven't breathed in all these years. The last time was in the hospital with Jean and with Miss Nightingale. And there's been no Jean to give me answers, a fact I have faced many times.

But if I couldn't find one nurse, perhaps I could find the other.

The balm I procured for Meg in Brighton – where is it now? All the things we gathered in our house to make it a home: where are the kitchen things, the books and bedding and socks and shoes belonging to the boys? She took such care of me – a dead man needs this more than most – and so did Agnes, who had a way of massaging my feet. On mornings after she'd performed as Cleopatra, or as Katherine, or hapless Susan, I let Agnes sleep and took care of her (bread, egg, kettle, tea). Then I ventured out into the streets of Eastbourne and headed for the water. The ocean remained attractive to me. The memory of the ship I took to the Crimea – most of that memory is lost. I was never a boy who cared greatly for ships or trains or bridges. But I do know I stood that day holding the ship's rail, waving at nobody in particular and therefore waving at everybody, breathing in and out. I was preparing my mind for the thrust and hurry of war, skipping ahead to the part where I would return home, barely scratched (it's an optimistic boy who cares for trees and birds and books). But inside my chest my heart must have been skidding and thumping.

A funny thing happens when Mabel comes past me in the doorway, holding a bucket: my hands shake, seem to itch for her. The bucket comes swinging towards my knees and she drives past me down the hall, then down the stairs. A loose, nonsense hum follows in the air.

From her bed, Miss Nightingale calls for Mabel, and the voice that comes out is nothing small or weak. When she summons her – *Mabel!* – it's a voice with the lid right off. I hear a bit of what they're saying, but mostly I try to shut my ears, to be a good person.

Then again, getting thrown out of the house won't matter to me. Police? I've had worse. I wander to a part of the wall in the hallway where there's a bench so I sit and sort of slump down, suddenly tired (always *suddenly tired*). If they're expecting me to run, or fight, those ladies don't know me at all. Better to close my eyes, to remember what it was to be normal and unbroken.

The hand that jolts me awake is Mabel's and again I receive the gift of her pleasing open face, round and soft.

'Come in,' Mabel says. 'She says to come in.'

I sit up. 'Will you stay?'

Mabel shakes her head. 'Miss Nightingale says just you. She doesn't have a lot of time.'

I enter the room, sit on the chair. I rub my legs, let my body and mind go *in-out, in-out*. Calmness surrounds me; a pair of lamps is aglow. She draws me closer. Her head favours one side, as if she is searching for something missing on her shoulder. What a presence, with the lace low over her forehead and the tidy squares of blankets across her knees. The breeze rushes in and I wonder how long I will last in this draughty room. I know she never married; I know she worked and was a recluse. *Me too*, I want to say. *I, too, am done with people.* I wonder what has kept her alive this long. Time is cracking apart, here in her house.

'What is your name again?'

'Silas.' I bring my palm to my chest, to the place.

'Yes. That's right.'

She peers at me with clouds in her eyes and I figure that she is blind or nearly blind. However: a mistake to think she cannot see exactly what has happened to me.

I start in a whisper. 'Miss Nightingale, why have I been wandering all these years? I haven't been able to die. Neither have you.'

She has turned from me.

'Jean was the last person I saw,' I say. 'She was in the room when I died.'

'So was I.'

'Yes, I know. Something went wrong, didn't it.'

She meets my gaze again. 'I don't remember.'

'I think you do.' *In-out, in-out.* I plunge onwards. 'I loved her, and I told her I loved her in that room.'

A shadow crosses her face. 'Do you know what happened to you before then?'

'I'd been shot.'

Miss Nightingale churns her legs beneath the blankets and presses down at her sides as though to get up. She isn't a slip of a thing, and I recognise the effort and the ghost of her strength in her arms. I want to ask how she feels. Do we feel the same?

'Bleeding, I remember,' she says. 'Inside the heart, and a cardiac tamponade. Very risky.'

I think of Jean and what might have been going through her mind as I lay on the surgeon's table. The address I'd written on that bit of paper – had she kept it?

'And Jean wanted to help?' I ask.

'She did. But it was not her place. It was foolish.'

My head races and my skin fizzes. The world outside

Miss Nightingale's chamber and beyond the window shrinks. My life is a series of rooms and I am back at the barracks – really, truly there with her again in those final moments. In fifty-five years I have not found her in any other room on earth.

'What did she do?'

'Son, it will not help.'

'Tell me.'

'I might not remember.'

'Please,' I say. 'Try.'

'Jean wanted you alive. So she reached out. She ... touched you. She put her hand on your heart.'

In-out. 'And the surgeon had said there was no hope of my survival.'

'That's correct.'

'So she was trying to save me.'

Miss Nightingale twists the edge of a blanket. Fingers bent and gnarled, her eyes swimming and unfocused. 'That's what she said. But she might have killed you.'

I need to steady myself. I try to know my heart and its sensations when Jean was there with her lovely hands. I am searching with my mind but coming up short. I see Miss Nightingale's chest rise and fall. I sense agitation behind her eyelids.

'And what happened to her then?'

For the longest time she says nothing. 'Lots of nurses had ideas in their heads. Some broke the rules.'

'Was she punished?'

She nods, once. 'She was dismissed.'

'You sent her away?'

'I can tell you're not a man who knows what it is to have a temper.'

Tears are now raining inside me. 'But she was right to try – can't you see that? It almost worked,' I say. 'I almost lived.'

Jean

St James's, London
April 1861

A cool and drizzly afternoon, the sky a squirrel-grey. Jean waited across the road from the memorial. She stared at the three guardsmen cast in bronze, up high on stone blocks, their heads bowed. Above them on a plinth, the figure of a cloaked woman had her arms outstretched. On the street Jean counted thirty or so people milling around. Some had umbrellas and others let the faint rain fall upon them while they smoked and talked. A lady in a dress with long green sleeves and a lace bonnet made her way through the crowd, leading a little brown dog on a leash. A group of men Jean's age crossed the Mall in front of her, some in top hats and bowler hats, their hands in their dark sack jackets. Against the dull background of Waterloo Place a man in a scarlet British army coat stood out, and Jean was stung by pinpricks near her heart – of desire, of sadness, of grief. The man, who did not notice her watching, was far taller than Silas, and a proud and robust energy came from him as he dashed in front of a carriage and joined the group at the monument. She recalled Silas, buried at Scutari, and the rich crimson wool of his uniform, likely burnt to prevent disease.

Seeing the soldier in red, feeling the rain on her shoulders: a decision. She would continue the courtship with Walter. She would go again to his house, not tonight but soon. He was away visiting his father but had told Jean both the date and the day of the week he'd return on the train, and it was as if he was underlining the words in pen. She had never nursed Walter at Scutari and he didn't need her to do that now. When she caressed his face and the soft part of his elbow where his arm ended, they understood each other. Sometimes he made jokes, sometimes he didn't, and with Walter the twin charges of desire and hunger could be rounded out nicely. A walk with him through the high grass of Clapham Common. Tea at his modest flat, where he lived alone. The fearful thrill of spying her name, just once, in a letter last week he had written to his father.

Crossing the street with her basket on her arm and becoming a part of the crowd of strangers, Jean waited for something to start. She'd expected a stage, speeches, perhaps a prayer or a ribbon or a white sheet draped over the top like icing. But all she saw was a pair of workmen scuttling around the corners of the monument, polishing the bronze reliefs with rags. Rose's husband knew a newspaper man – perhaps that bearded gentleman on the corner, with paper and pencil – who'd told him it would be unveiled at two o'clock. The new monument to the Crimean War at Waterloo Place, five years after the last remnants of the British Army had straggled home.

'What do you think? Ma'am, any thoughts?'

It was the man with the notepad, now at her elbow.

'It's more arresting than I thought it would be,' she replied. 'It feels powerful.'

In truth it left her a little cold. She'd expected a sense of pride, a flicker of recognition. She did feel fondness for the faces of the soldiers, the way the sculptor had captured their smooth skin and sombre expressions. They were life-sized and imposing but the fabric of their coats appeared plush enough to touch. Jean didn't recognise the figure of the woman at the top. Perhaps it was a goddess, with haloes of leaves that circled her wrists. At that moment, Jean recalled the séance she attended last summer, where a woman had brought a daguerreotype of a girl with a wreath in her hair. Jean's first and only séance, surrounded by a dozen other people, mostly mothers and lovers – lost mothers, lost lovers. The room was velvety, the atmosphere febrile. Jean envied that one lady with the image of her daughter; she felt a dark pain that other people had their folded drawings and tiny portraits painted inside lockets, sacred souvenirs of loved ones who had gone to the other side and might still be – what? Listening? Waiting? Searching too? One father cradled his son's hat, seeming to urge it up into the air (*Take it, take it!*) but Jean owned no charcoal sketch of Silas's face, nothing at all belonging to him, and why couldn't they have allowed her a moment in the dead house – to see him one last time, if nothing else. A silly idea to go to the séance – a garden shed in Hoxton, the curtains drawn and thick white candles on a table in the centre – clutching only Silas's fading words on their slip of paper. But once Jean had an idea in her head, it was hard to ignore, and surely it couldn't hurt. No harm in it.

Ghosts everywhere.

But she hadn't sensed a thing.

Then: a sound like a bullet dropped into a pan. She jumped. He was still there. The newspaper man bent to pick up a key from the ground.

She composed herself and raised an arm towards the other statue. 'Who do you think that is?'

'The lady?' he asked. 'She stands for honour or victory, I've been told. I don't think she's anybody in particular.'

Jean had read about Florence Nightingale in the newspaper. She had been in that place for eighteen months longer than Jean. She had surprised her family upon returning from the Crimea, walking across the fields to their country house. Miss N had met the Queen and the Queen had given her a brooch. But no statue. Miss N was now rather sick – Jean had read that too.

Cold as stone, Jean remembered the words of the tailor when she was buying her uniforms: *Women can't imagine that sort of suffering.*

'Those are wreaths,' he said. 'Laurel leaves.'

Jean said, 'My husband served in the army, in the 97th Regiment. That's why I'm here.'

'Oh, is that so?' Was that curiosity on the journalist's face? Scepticism?

'But he was shot and died. He remains buried in the east, near Constantinople.'

'That's a terrible tragedy, ma'am, I'm sorry.'

Jean nodded. *Had* she really been a nurse there?

'I thought there would be speeches, didn't you? Something official?' she said.

The man agreed. 'I've been here since noon. I think they've forgotten you all.'

'Easy to do.' Jean smiled. 'Excuse me for a moment.'

He held up his pencil. 'Sorry, if you have time, I might gather a few more of your thoughts. May I ask: what was your husband's name?'

But Jean was already moving away. She walked to the side of the monument and held one of her palms against the granite. She reached up and ran her fingers across the word *Crimea* etched into the unfeeling stone.

At least she wouldn't be late. Two o'clock had become three o'clock and now with the sky clearing and the rain gone, the journalist and the lady with the dog and the soldier in red all disappeared, Jean left the memorial on its little island surrounded by busy streets and headed south to St James's Park.

Anna was on a bench, waiting for her.

Tender to reunite after all these years, tender even on this, their fourth visit since Jean wrote to the Turners eight months ago after catching sight of an ageing but hearty-looking Mr Turner at Hyde Park Corner. Jean had frozen to the spot but worked up the courage, later, to write. He'd passed the letter on to Anna, he said, who would be happy to see her old governess. Nothing else in the letter from him, which was fine, Jean told herself. It was fine. Painful to talk about how much time had passed, and so Jean never spoke of Benjamin unless Anna brought him up, which wasn't often. Jean had vowed never to return to the house, because what would be the point of that? But if Mr Turner would allow Anna to cross the park one afternoon to meet her – or perhaps if he would accompany his daughter, a suggestion he was yet to heed – it would make Jean very happy.

Anna, becoming so grown up with her thick blonde hair parted and pulled back under lace. She was pretty in her bonnet and yellow dress, and nearly Jean's height. Jean found that her voice choked a little. She shielded her face from the sun, tried to wave away the tears while she sat beside Anna on the park bench. From her basket she pulled out a parcel.

'On the occasion of your sixteenth birthday,' she said, adding, before Anna could correct her: 'Yes, next week, I know.'

'Thank you, Miss Frawley.' Anna took the bundle wrapped in silver paper. 'You must tell me when your birthday is, so I can buy you a gift.'

'Oh, I don't need anything,' she said, brushing down her skirt. She plucked a blade of grass from her lap. 'Birthdays are for children.'

'But presents are such fun!'

'As I said: for children. I'm practically twice your age.'

'That doesn't seem possible.' Anna was focused on the unwrapping. It was a bracelet of black beads, and seeing it in Anna's palm and then on her wrist made Jean very happy. She'd chosen well. She took out a second paper parcel – two lemon cakes, which she set on the bench.

'I love it – thank you.'

'You're welcome. Very smart on you.'

'Are these beads meant for good luck?'

'I'd say that they are.'

Anna fondled the bracelet. 'The twins will want to play with them.'

Jean was stricken. 'Oh, yes, not near their mouths. How are the twins?'

'Fat. Grubby. Noisy. Spoilt.'

'Beautiful.'

'Yes. And beautiful. May I?'

Jean motioned at the food. 'Ha. Yes. Have both if you like.'

Sixteen years old: Jean had some understanding of Anna's sweet mind opening up to the world. And yet she was still a child, diving un-daintily into the lemon cake. Anna would have linen dresses, dances, banquets; Jean undid any notion in her head that their experience of being sixteen would be similar. But perhaps they could be braided together somewhat from now. She could even confide in the girl about her ambition. In her experience children like Anna accepted ideas unrelated to their own lives quite mildly.

'Anna, do you remember I said I went away and learnt to be a nurse?'

'Yes! During the war. What was it like?'

'Well. Parts of it were good. But it also broke my heart.'

Anna was still. Then she edged closer and rested her head on Jean's shoulder.

Jean set her eyes forward onto a path that bent through the park. 'I think I'd like to become a doctor.' The simplicity and rightness of saying it aloud.

'Can you do that?' Anna took another nibble of cake.

'Do you think I should try?'

She shrugged. 'Mummy says it's the most important thing.'

Florence

Risky, risky, risky. God took a risk on me. Father took a risk on me. So too Sidney Herbert and the men in the War Office. Girls like Jean can be nurses now because of me. But still I am faced with the soldiers who come creeping through the walls and down from the ceiling to meet me in the darkness of my room. And some of those haunting me have been nurses, the light gone from their eyes because of what they've seen. And a few mothers (I always said mothers were the nurses of their own homes) who have lost children to tuberculosis or scarlet fever, diphtheria or whooping cough – sometimes I see them. I tried to give advice in those books over there, and now thousands read my words. Sanitation was a good start. Ventilation. Warmth, diet, sunlight. But that was not all. Too many children die because they have no mother or nurse or doctor to help them.

Things could have been different with Jean, which I knew even as I sent her away. (Oh, her face when she reached into the chest cavity! Like that of a thieving child!) Her defiance, her reticence around me, but also her curiosity and gentleness and respect. Now I see that she was rather like my feline friends – thwarting my expectations with her intelligence, her strength of will. Jean has visited me only in my dreams, has never needed to haunt me in this room. I try to smile. I lick my lips and rub my eyes. She was happy to go to the dead house. I know she would do it again.

I'm in my own foreign country and I want to be sure of a few things before I go. The year is 1910 and how surprising that I've lived to see it. The speed of change and the scale of it all take my breath away. My view out onto the street has altered with each passing year and when I turn away from the window to face my bedroom more sounds creep in than ever before. Tiny things make the most noise. Rats and vermin will find their way into your quarters and rummage around on the pillow behind your head in the middle of the night. Here, see, the rat perched on my chest? It shows me its black eyes and it paws at the front of my apron, telling me to *wake up!* I must have fallen asleep and the soldiers will be wondering where I am. They'll be eager to catch me on my rounds. Parthe is waiting for me downstairs at the pianoforte, driving a single finger onto a key over and over. Cockroaches will get between the men's toes, and silverfish will wriggle across the floor in the early hours of the morning. If she doesn't get out of the house soon, my loving sister will die of the shock of it all. Nothing has prepared her for this!

If I rise out of bed now, I can do my rounds. Up. Up. Up! Four miles of beds with rats perched on the pillows of every man, alive or dead. There's only a foot and a half between each bed, and just when I'm working my way between two beds, I get stuck, unable to shift my legs and free myself. This noise I'm making, out of my mouth, will wake up that patient, and that one, and that one. Silence is a virtue when a patient is in distress, Parthe, and you must stop that playing at once. See here? The man with his face half gone. His bad side is wrapped up, so I don't have to worry about Parthe being afraid. The other half of his face is smooth and handsome, perfect, like an egg. The sheet is pulled up to his neck and he's tucked in like a newborn babe. His eyes are searching mine and, oh, yes, I know what he wants.

Home.

Home is the word in our dreams. It grows even here, outside in the grounds of the barracks, pushing up through the mud and the frost, growing where nothing else does. The word is a boiled sweet on the tongue, honey on bread, and Mother will come to dole it out in spoonfuls for being such good girls! So patient while we wait for home.

But, Parthe, while you and I have been circling the beds, searching for a way out, I suspect that home has been replaced and we are not welcome in it. When we get back to Lea Hurst I fear the curtains will be different, the trees on the great green lawn denuded, the birds dropped out of the sky, our toys and prayer books not where we left them. What was your favourite prayer when we were children? I know that you worshipped less and you thought me different because of my devotion, but you were a good girl who listened in church. Back then our favourite prayers were the ones that mentioned *angel* or *offspring* or *mother* or *breast*. If only I could remember your best prayer I might be able to say it now and become unstuck. The man in the bandages has fallen asleep and the rat's eyes have become warm and loving towards me. I will say my own favourite prayer now, while I'm being watched.

Silas

Mabel enters the room. She stands behind me. Together we watch the sleeping figure on the bed. There – her *in-out, in-out*. Barely. So gentle.

'Why have you come?' Mabel whispers. 'What have you been doing all these years, really?'

'I've been in the churchyard where my parents are buried.'

'You loved your parents.'

'I've had even longer to miss them now. That's been cruel,' I say. 'And my house in the village is the address I wrote down for Jean to come find me. I wondered if she might.'

I take in the belongings of a rich lady, a long life of accumulation and stability and adventure. Her head is turned away from Mabel and me, towards the window, her eyes closed.

'And what did you do there for all those years?' Mabel asks softly. I cannot see her face.

'I climbed the hill behind the churchyard. I picked flowers and kept my parents' headstones clean. I liked to read the headstones of other people. I imagined what mine might say, if I had one. People came and went – whole families across the years. I would lie in the grass and watch the seasons change.'

'And did Jean ever visit?'

'She didn't. I never saw her.' *She reached in and touched my heart.*

'And why are you here now?'

'A sense of time that I haven't had before. The world is changing around me.'

My terrible loneliness all these years – it lifts in a brief moment. Flesh cleaving to flesh. Headstones in the moonlight and me alone in the churchyard, seeing the candles and lights of the village go out, one by one. Me, in the dead house, hearing voices then nothing at all. In a flash, the thought I've held on to for years: that Jean has indeed been on this earth and parallel to me the whole time; I simply couldn't see.

Many minutes pass, so many that I assume Mabel has left the room without my hearing.

I say, 'She lived a long life.'

Miss Nightingale stirs, a sound like a purr coming from her throat. She does not wake.

Jean

Holsworthy, Devon
May 1894

She set out up the lane towards the Hazels' farm. Before leaving home she'd taken her bonnet from the back of the door and collected her battered black bag. The green cloth bundle was still inside, as well as Silas's note, though his handwriting had long faded from the page.

It was just after sunrise and a wash of yellow dappled the hedgerows and the trees. Jean was used to being watched and some days she considered herself the way others in the village might, measured herself through their lens. She was sixty-four years old, a little stooped and slowed by age. She had lost a lot of hair – she didn't care to know how much and so she rarely put a comb or brush to her skull. She had no appendix left and only half of the little finger on her right hand after an accident with a gate. (This had happened years before – a time when she worked in even greater secrecy. Heading in to see a patient, dawn light, feeling preoccupied, Jean opened the gate to the house and caught her finger in its wire latch. The memory, now, went *slam* into her. And with it came the face of the patient, a girl with green eyes, a girl in trouble, who needed Jean's help to bring on her monthly course. Herbs like pennyroyal or slippery elm or motherwort or juniper were often all the country girls had. And sometimes they failed. Jean had carried out the delicate procedure with her finger wrapped in a bandage, resisting all help.)

Now, Jean stood as tall as Mr Hazel's decrepit mare. She tightened the apron around her waist and felt a warm breeze spin itself around her. This early in summer and the puddles she saw last night coming back from the Hazels' house had already dried. In the village a man pushed a barrow piled with sacks, and at the fountain a pigeon fluttered, drops of water leaving its wings and kissing the pavement wet. Jean saw herself in the windows she passed and was caught with an affection for this woman she'd become but did not quite feel she was.

Had it really been that long?

Time had seemed endless. She'd once opened her home to paying boarders, two twenty-five-year-old men studying to be doctors, pupils at a Harley Street clinic. How she had pressed them for details. With the windows open to the evening air (Miss N would be pleased) she gave them extra servings of whatever she'd made in the big black pot to coax them to sit a while longer at dinnertime. Though kind, they barely knew her; their gaze going *through* her, she felt. They seemed to think her a dull and ordinary middle-aged woman who, yes, had once been a nurse under Nightingale, but they'd exhausted those questions pretty fast. In between forks scraping on plates and their clean-shaven jaws working away at the meat, they explained the lessons taken with real doctors and they answered Jean's questions: how the heart worked, the spleen, the liver. How to triangulate and tap to find an inflamed appendix. How to prise a recalcitrant baby from a woman stuck in labour. How to sedate a patient, how to stabilise a patient, how to wake one up.

How easily those two physicians-in-training spread out their large hands and pushed back from the table and went upstairs and fell into bed while Jean scrubbed the pans and ran through her mind all the knowledge they'd dropped like crumbs. She wanted to know and absorb their brains while they slept. In the kitchen, Jean kept on.

At the stable she set her black bag on the ground and knocked. The Hazel boy, Thomas, grinned when he saw her. His face was broad and pale as an onion.

She followed him as he plodded down the centre and popped into the stables. Jean counted four horses – two brown and two grey with patterns like white butterflies on their faces. Thomas moved swiftly between the animals in his care. He held a bucket of water and tipped it into the troughs. It was loving work. Thomas plunged his arms into sacks of feed, and Jean saw a wedge of carrot and scraps of cabbage and potato skins scattered on the messy floor. She felt struck in the chest: residual hunger and shame so visceral that surely a sensitive boy like Thomas would notice.

He smiled. 'They're very friendly today.'

She nodded and leant the back of her forearm against one of the horses, keeping her clean palms away from its dusty flank. 'How is your mother?'

Thomas shrugged. *So-so.* He patted the younger mare vigorously as though he could bury the bad news in her mane. 'She still hasn't eaten anything. A bit of water,' he added before Jean asked.

The grassy, sweaty stench of the stables, and the memory of the one from her childhood was called up so easily. Jean breathed it in. She tried to straighten her shoulders.

She forced her voice to sound bright. 'It's hard. The pain. Who feels like eating when they're poorly?'

'You'll go in to her? She was asking for you earlier, but she might be asleep now.'

'I will. Just coming to say hello and gather my thoughts.' Jean waved goodbye, then stepped back out into the dimly lit barn. Behind the doors Thomas moved. She caught sight of his brown shirt and afterwards the black-globe eye of the horse watching her leave.

A girl in a blue dress with a neat plait and narrow nose let her into the house and through to the room where Mrs Hazel was seated in the family's big chair. The girl was one of the Hazel daughters – Jean was no longer as sharp with names as she used to be. Days earlier this girl, or her almost identical sister, had learnt that Jean had been a Nightingale. Later she slipped Jean a tightly packed letter about her own nursing ambitions, filled with questions about the sort of person Miss N had been. How extraordinary to Jean that she should be older than all the people in this house. When she encountered girls like this one, or recalled her own daughter, Millie, at this age, she couldn't help thinking, *I used to be like you.* It was not a distressing thought, or a jealous one, just disbelief. Once when she'd been teaching Millie how to cover a pillow in a cotton slip, she recalled being a five-year-old girl herself with her fingers on the clean white corners, learning the trick from her own mother. Jean remembered Walter teaching an older Millie how to prune the delphiniums – perhaps, in that moment, he felt the same. *How did I get here?*

Jean rapped lightly on the doorframe. 'Good morning, Mrs Hazel.' The woman's energy had been solid and intimidating before she became ill. Mrs Hazel said little, but when she had something forceful and insistent to convey, she liked to clutch at her son, her neighbours, Jean herself.

When she saw her in the centre of the room, Jean was touched by the square of cloth that Mrs Hazel's arm rested on – it reminded Jean of a baby blanket she'd kept in a drawer after Millie was born. Mrs Hazel had six children. Thomas was the youngest and sweetest, and perhaps it was a blanket he'd fetched.

'I saw Thomas in the barn. He said you'd taken some water.'

As though the woman had spoken, Jean continued, 'Water is good, let's see if we can't get you to have some more before I leave. I understand not wanting to eat anything.' Jean persisted with the patter, low but firm so Mrs Hazel didn't have to strain to hear.

Mrs Hazel kept her eyes shut but she waved in greeting and then returned her hand to the site of the pain. Jean saw again the too-large mound of the woman's stomach. She understood many of the wonders of the body and its craven mistakes. Mrs Hazel looked as if she were five or six months pregnant even though she was fifty-one, nearly fifty-two, and this was no baby. Sometimes the words of Miss N came to her – expressions such as *Risky, risky, risky*. But also words about sunlight, air, decisiveness.

'You have, I think, Mrs Hazel, a large abscess that is causing you great discomfort. Hard to know whether it is anything more sinister than fluid, but I tend to think not.'

With some difficulty Mrs Hazel replied, 'Like a cow. We've had to drain them before.'

'Exactly like that,' Jean said.

'I hope not exactly like that.'

Jean laughed kindly.

Mrs Hazel winced, and from the back of her throat came a whimper that she muffled with a rag clenched against her mouth. The room had been cleared since Jean was last here, merely hours ago. Fresh blankets were folded on the sideboard and the windows were open to the air. On a stool across from Mrs Hazel, where she could see clearly without having to shift her neck, was a vase of golden daffodils. She was a farmer's wife, a farmer herself, and Jean thought she'd probably never spent more than a week in bed since having her children. This sort of news must be hard to take.

Jean made her way to Mrs Hazel's side and put down her bag. 'I'm going to examine you now, if that's all right.'

Mrs Hazel shifted onto her left side in the chair and thrust a cushion out of her way and onto the floor. The poor woman cried for a moment now, a sharp sob, but that too was stoppered up with the rag to her mouth. Her skin was awash with sweat and her face was the colour of straw. Carefully, Jean kneaded Mrs Hazel's belly and saw how she kept her eyes away from the site of the distress, something she'd noticed half the soldiers do. (The other half stared as best they could, fascinated by the surgeon's blade, the bandage going up and down a limb. What had become of the soaked compress that had gone in and out of Silas's wound?)

'I'll ask you to breathe as normally as you can.'

Mrs Hazel, looking squarely at Jean, whispered, 'Yes, Doctor.' Even though they both knew she wasn't.

Jean thought of Thomas brushing down the horses, the girl out in the kitchen who wanted to be a nurse, the other grown-up boys at work with Mr Hazel in the fields beyond the barn. It was a fragile line between life and death. On one side: a blade, some fluid. Nothing in between.

Florence

My body is a rectangle, a circle, a heart. My bed is a boat. The ceiling is a mountain beside the sea. My hands are very soft, which doesn't seem right. No, they're hard and rough – see all the things I do for these men, all the things I've solved? God called me to do good in the world, though it took me years to understand what that would be. It isn't enough to say they would be nothing without me, without these ladies here. We don't exist for them, not really. My hands are writing a letter that I started when I was born but the words are not here yet and the words are written in stone. My hands are designing pavilions, my hands are stirring broth, I am doing sums in ledgers. My hands are useless to these men, chopped off, somewhere.

Outside, the light shimmers and, oh, I'll miss that street

and its passers-by with their bell-voices floating up to my window. The dogs of the neighbourhood scatter themselves across the stones and return to one another, their snouts nudging point to point like drifting bergs. Now the glare is on my face and I'm kicking away from the shore, my dear little owl on my shoulder. Do we know how to sail?

The first men were felled like trees while the sun turned overhead – *Mabel? Are you there?* The first men whose faces I can recall sat at a long table topped with candles and flowers and one of them was discussing the war, and would I help?

'Mabel?' Where is she?

Where's the young lady Jean? I sent her away when I had the fever. I will be better by daybreak and then she will return. Obedient girl, she closed the door behind her. How illuminating it is to be left alone.

Where's the man? Should have stuck a pin in him to see if he was real.

Lived long.

Loved well.

Raked muck.

Hemmed bones.

'Jean?' A thud now. That must be her. That must be my mother at the fence. That must be her on the stairs; she's come for me. The light is in my eyes again; it is my friend. The light is feeding me as though I were a plant.

Tore skin.

Pressed blood.

Grew twisted.
Stood tall.
Ached lengthways.
Home dreamt.

I lie with my feet at the wrong end of the bed. A kitten pops itself over my legs and back again. I lie with some other faces in the room, the sick men all around. I tore skin, I stood tall, I saw their faces.

Ah, yes, the soldier has come back and I'm guilty, of course I'm guilty. I've been confessing since I was thirty-six years old. They thought I knew nothing and then they thought I knew everything. They were never to blame. Mother had to follow me around afterwards to make sure I didn't say anything too strange. And she never mentioned Malvern or my time in the asylum, even though part of me very much wanted her to ask me precisely what had happened to me. Would have preferred her to come right out and say it.

Why won't Mabel come right out and say it?

Chopped limbs.
Opened windows.
Streaming light and air.

The man Silas is here wanting, needing something from me. Answers, sure, but he has a look in his eye that suggests his time has come. I never was good at telling this time in men's eyes – I'll admit other nurses were better at it. Swore they could see a veil lifting, a suck of air out of the room, an unusual and unsettling silence, right before a person breathed their last. Silas here is different, telling me that he *hibernates*. Which is new to me and not anything a man has uttered before. Telling Mabel that months go by, usually in winter, where he seems to fall asleep in one place then wake up in another, new and fresh. And all the while in the churchyard too.

A life of people wanting things from me. Holding up bodies is women's work. A woman can go to bed alone and wake with a sleeping husband beside her, a child tucked up by her breast, all aloneness gone from her body without her knowing quite when. Being ill buys one some time, a sense of control, solitude. (I have heard that an unmarried lady might become a nun so she can't be summoned home whenever her family gets bored or lonely or spiritless. In taking her vows she has rejected the tyranny of being available. Her mind is her own. All those decades ago, during that lush time in Rome, I could see the appeal.)

Once I was alone with a soldier in the Barrack Hospital. I had hours to help him through the night. I changed his bedclothes and told him silly lies about what his body might be able to overcome. No shame in that. But I was exhausted and it felt as though God Himself was inside my brain, giving me slices of clarity, feeding me the lines so that nothing I said felt bad or wrong. It was God saying goodbye to this man, God reassuring him what tomorrow would be like, that the man – despite his vicious injuries – would again see the rising sun. He had lost half an arm below the elbow and half a leg below the knee, and one side of his face was a great hole that I'd carefully wrapped with gauze and here it really did resemble a child's doll, sorely loved. He was his mother's boy, once, in a different land. And he was being unmade before my eyes. All the while this tugging, from God, inside. The fatigue in me rubbed up against my guilt (it was never far away, no matter what I said about it) and all of God's words came spilling out, from me to him, the silence all around when neither of us spoke. His mouth made its ghastly sound and my heart reached for him. Not yet twenty-two.

Countless boys like that – alone with God and me in the lamp-lit hours.

And what's this? A sound is coming from the roof of the world. I've been dreaming and the sound is hauling me up, a fish with a hook in my great drooping mouth. Why won't it let me stay? The hook isn't big, or shiny, or sharp. I can fight it, I'm sure. And why all this noise? Why all this rushing, blooming, the hole in my bedroom wall like a cloud opening up to let my good thoughts out into the street? These are private thoughts! A private bedroom! Nobody comes here except for Mabel and Dr Thorne, or is it Dr Keith? That soldier Silas must have forced his way in. Such a shame, he seemed so peaceful. So much warring among men and yet he appears different from them all. Coming in gentle. He appears to me like a son.

And didn't I say something to Mabel about no more visitors? And didn't I say to Mabel that I need time to get my thoughts in order, every single one? The thoughts of my life are like an enormous knotted scarf, each knot a prayer. A knot for the time I watched a surgeon's silver saw go through a white thigh bone like an eclipse, *snicker-snack*. A knot for when I strolled with Parthe at Claydon House and chose flowers for the vase in the room she kept for me there, a knot for Mother's loving hand on my waist at the Doveton train station platform when I was ten years old and the carriages were rushing past, a knot for each time Papa clapped while I chanted in my lessons *erratum, errata*. A knot for the time I was sixteen, walking in the garden, and God first revealed Himself to me. The hole in the wall grows bigger still. One of the men who wanted to marry me pitches into my vision. A knot for the time a gentleman was guiding me into a theatre to watch a play but I'd done something to disappoint him, said the wrong thing. And he pinched me on the underside of my arm as though I were a child.

I cannot take it all with me. The man who is my son – just my luck! Here he is! *Hello!* My mind gapes at his mind. *Please close the wall!* The light is too sharp and the draught is too draughty. *Son?* I need everything back inside, in boxes, on the ship. Closed up and ready for travel.

His voice finds me now. A beautiful voice, deep and slow and sad. 'Miss Nightingale?'

I yawn an answer back to him, sending it out through the wide expanse of my skull. *You take the boxes, I'll hold the rail.*

Ah. Good boy. He seems to hear me because now he makes his way to the wall where the huge hole shimmers. Outside, the world of the street shouts to me. I'm lucky to still have some of my senses. My hearing, though, is going (oh, I'd love to hear a sparrow). I listen for the growl of motor cars and the steady rhythm of hansom cabs on the summer tar and the bony footfalls of horses. It could all send me to sleep again.

With a flick Silas leans his weight on the sash, down, and the noises disappear, the hole and the sad brief pinching memory and the scarf whipping away like a heavy bird – gone, sailed off into the wind.

And then he is beside me and I'm turning my face towards him. It isn't difficult to listen, though, because his words are reaching me effortlessly in that feathered way I remember as a girl. A feeling at the edge of my mind. Fragile.

I shiver.

Likely to slip away.

'Let me tell you what it's like,' he says.

Epilogue

Well, the washing still needed doing. But first Mabel sent for the doctor and the undertaker. The lady doctor who turned up, knocking, and then the two gentlemen who followed on the steps behind, very much wanted to talk about the great and extraordinary Florence Nightingale.

Afterwards, Mabel shut the door and went upstairs to gather the bedclothes from Florence's room. Yesterday, in the late hours of the afternoon, she had spent time staring at Florence. Mabel was not her daughter or granddaughter so she hadn't lingered on the old lady's face when she was alive, on the narrow nose and eyes, lost to it all now. Mabel would never see those features again.

She took in the dresser one last time and again found piles of envelopes and letters bound in string. Propped up were pictures of the Karnak temple in Egypt, the ruins of a castle in Germany, St Peter's Basilica, an engraving of the frescoes of Rome. In the corner of one frame Miss Nightingale had tucked a faded line drawing, the size of a postage stamp, of an owl.

Her job in this fine house was not Mabel's first, nor would it be her last, and she knew enough about Florence to be sure she would have resented someone fawning over her. Better for Mabel to go about her business efficiently and calmly.

In time, Mabel too would grow old. She gathered a loose scrap of sheet and pushed it into the bundle, holding herself taut, feeling the sun through Florence's window.

But! Not anytime soon.

She observed the smooth skin on her arms and her springiness while she resumed her work, pulling open the sash window. Years away. Hadn't she and Silas understood each other *because* of all the years she had left? She believed every word that man had said.

And now she must go on.

Do the washing.

Call the newspapers.

Put away the butter.

Box up the spinach and onions and cherries. She would take them with her.

It was summer.

No breeze stirred. No birds sang.

She knew doctors made an oath that said, *First, do no harm*. But still it wouldn't be right to tell them about the man lying dead in the back garden of Florence's house. The undertaker and his assistant had certainly not asked if there was a second corpse that needed taking care of. And so Silas's body lay among the freesias and dahlias in the corner of the yard.

He had said how lucky he was to find her. That she was special. And, no, he wasn't the only person to have told her this, but she would keep his words close for all time.

But first! She would step out into the city. This was 1910 – a clean and narrow year. Just a few smart, slim marks on the page. *1910*. Lean and light and nothing to fear. Her father had been a printer. Her mother was a seamstress. Mabel would buy the meat for tonight's supper – on Florence's purse – because who knew where she would be living in a week or so. She could fill the house with the smell of pastry and gravy one final time. Silas would be hungry forever. Mabel had heard of ancient tribes leaving pots of preserved apricots, parcels of rice and cinnamon sticks in the crooks of newly dead kings' arms. Florence had told her this.

Mabel believed them both. All of it.

She got her basket and the household purse from its spot in the low cupboard. At the end of the garden she stooped to meet Silas's face. His eyes were closed. In death, his cheeks and nose and chin had softened. His flesh was the colour of bandages, and when she touched the hair on his head, it came from another world. She snatched her hand away.

After a time, she put down her things and lay beside him. She fitted her short body beside his longer one, her face at his shoulder, her knees pressing against his trousers. She caught some of his coldness while she lay on the lawn. Florence had been a rich child, living in an enormous house with cooks and governesses and gardeners. But the one thing Florence always said she missed in her old age was her bare skin against the warm green grass.

Author's note

In 2022, in a shop in Oxford, I found a second-hand copy of *Florence Nightingale: The Woman and Her Legend* by Mark Bostridge. This brilliant biography opened up my novel for me. I'm also indebted to the following titles: *Florence Nightingale at First Hand* by Lynn McDonald; *Tormented Hope: Nine Hypochondriac Lives* by Brian Dillon; *A Brief History of Florence Nightingale: And Her Real Legacy, a Revolution in Public Health* by Hugh Small; and *Florence Nightingale: The Making of a Radical Theologian* by Val Webb (and thanks to Ruth Delbridge for lending it to me several years ago). The epigraph 'Struggle must make a noise' is a line that Florence wrote in her diary in 1851. It is quoted in Webb's book and elsewhere. Some additional research came from the books *Florence Nightingale* by Lytton Strachey and

Crimea by Orlando Figes. I'm grateful to the staff at the Florence Nightingale Museum in London, and at Claydon House in the Aylesbury Vale. Special thanks to a National Trust volunteer at Claydon House who first told me the story about Athena the owl. All mistakes and forays into fiction are mine.

I wrote this book, over several years, on the lands of the Yuggera and Turrbal peoples, the Quandamooka people, the Bunjalung people, and the Gundungurra and Dharug peoples. I acknowledge their ongoing custodianship and sovereignty.

Acknowledgements

My special thanks to Aviva Tuffield for her belief in me and this novel, for her loyalty, patience, wisdom and support. I'm eternally grateful to Ian See for his generous edits, attentiveness and ideas. Thanks to that other Jean, my kind and diligent publicist, Jean Smith. Thanks also to Sarah Valle, Vanessa Pellatt, Cathy Vallance and Madeline Byrne for their time. It's a pleasure working with the whole team at UQP.

I was awarded a Varuna Residential Fellowship to write this novel; my thanks to the judges and all the staff. Every time I go to Varuna I'm inspired by my fellow writers and their ideas and friendship. Thanks also to Creative Australia for the generous grant to work on this manuscript, and Stephen Carleton and Bronwyn Lea at the Centre for Critical and Creative Writing at the University of Queensland for giving me office space as writer-in-residence, back in 2021. Their early belief in my project meant so much.

Thank you to Fiona Stager and Kevin Guy for giving me a place to write, and all the friendly faces at Avid Reader in West End. Thanks to my friends and work colleagues for their encouragement and enthusiasm (years of it!). I'm especially grateful to: Sean Di Lizio, Sikwasa van Zutphen, Andrea Baldwin, Jessica Miller, Ashley Hay and Yen-Rong Wong. High-five to Anthony Mullins for helping me solve a major plot point over a sandwich at New Farm Deli. I'm grateful to Tegan Bennett Daylight for her suggestions, and Sue White for her notes on surgery.

Robbie Arnott, Gail Jones, Kris Kneen and Emily Maguire read my manuscript and made my year with their endorsements. I admire these authors very much and thank them sincerely. Josh Durham designed a stunning cover for me. I'm so grateful for his vision and talent.

For their time, feedback, ideas, hard truths, above-and-beyond-ness, friendship and love, I thank Emma Doolan, Kate Zahnleiter, Kathy George, Sarah Kanake, Kris Kneen and Laura Jean McKay. And I could not have written this book without Mirandi Riwoe by my side, on the texts, in my corner.

Biggest thanks to Lenore, Peter, Jiselle, Simon, Harriet and Theo ♥ Endless gratitude for loving me as a daughter, sister, wife, mum and writer.